TO HELEN BACK

An utterly charming cozy mystery

SUSAN MCBRIDE

Helen Evans Investigates Book 1

JOFFE BOOKS

Revised edition 2024
Joffe Books, London
www.joffebooks.com

First published by Witness Impulse
in Great Britain in 2014

This paperback edition was first published
in Great Britain in 2024

Cover art by Dee Dee Book Covers

ISBN: 978-1-83526-423-2

Dedicated to the memory of my grandmother Helen,
whose love of puzzles and mysteries inspired me
to bring Helen Evans to life on the page.

CHAPTER ONE

Milton Grone woke up that Thursday morning much as he did every other.

As soon as the sun bumped above the horizon, tinting blue the morning sky, he rolled out of bed, careful, so as not to disturb his wife Shotsie who preferred not to rise at quite so early an hour.

She'd tugged the sheets from him sometime in the night and they twisted around her plump limbs. Corkscrews of blond framed a moon-shaped face and kewpie doll mouth from which rumbled a parade of snores.

Milt smiled smugly as he looked her over. She was his second wife and, at 43, younger than him by two decades. His first marriage had crumbled ten years before. He scowled at the thought of Delilah and their ungrateful pair of teenage kids.

He hadn't the slightest idea how the first bride he'd wed all those years before could have turned into such a shrew. She'd called him a tightwad and a cheater, cursing him loudly enough for all two hundred inhabitants of nosy River Bend, Illinois, to hear. He thought he'd gotten rid of her for good, but she wouldn't let go, coming after him for what she claimed was unpaid child support. The wretched woman thought she could scare him with threats of lawyers and lawsuits.

Milt scratched his jaw, figuring she had another thing coming if she thought he'd give in as easy as that.

With a snort, he pushed away from the sagging mattress and shuffled into the bathroom to shave and dress. He emerged five minutes after, clad in jeans and an undershirt faded to drab. Leaving Shotsie in bed, he slipped through the cock-eyed screened door and stepped out onto the porch.

He could already hear the noises of the town waking up: the bark of dogs from neighboring yards; the crunch of tires on the graveled road as the ponytailed paperboy whipped through his route; and a whistling from next door that struck him as far too cheerful for so early in the morning.

Milt growled, spitting into the dirt, knowing instantly from whose lips the perky tune emanated. He moved toward the fence in his bare feet and there, just beyond, he spotted the guilty bird.

Her back to him, she bent over a tangle of raspberry bushes, her slip peeking out beneath the hem of her duster. A straw hat ringed with yellow ribbon covered her head, tipping this way and that, as she splashed the contents of a watering can upon the bushes. A shovel lay nearby, its spade damp with fresh earth. She'd been out since the crack of dawn, no doubt, planting and whistling like a senile whippoorwill.

"Would you stop that god awful racket?" he begged, unable to keep silent a minute longer. He leaned his arms over the split-rail fence he'd built barely a week ago. "People are sleeping, old woman. It's just seven o'clock in the morning, in case your watch broke."

The water ceased pouring.

The stooped body in the flower-print housedress righted itself. The straw hat topped head swiveled.

"Are you speaking to me, Milton Grone?" she asked, the faint British clip still evident even though its bite had worn down.

What could be seen of her features hardly beamed at him with friendship. Instead, the age-spotted skin settled into hard lines. Thin lips pressed together.

If looks could kill, Milton thought, the old broad would have done him in right there on the spot. "You got your girdle on too tight today, grandma?" he asked, chuckling. "You sure aren't acting very neighborly."

"And you are?" Felicity Timmons' already high-pitched voice soared. She stood with her feet apart, shaking the watering can at him. "I would scarcely call your actions cordial," she said, splashing water about. "You run your lawn mower at all hours. You park that bloody truck of yours on the edge of the lot across the road so that no one can pass without nicking my prized Queen Elizabeth roses! And then there's the matter of that fence—"

"This fence?" Milton lifted up his arms and glanced down.

"Yes, of course, that fence!" Felicity's face reddened further. Her whole body shook. "You built it on my property!"

"The hell I did!"

"Six inches, to be exact! I've had Art Beaner from the board over here myself to check with his own eyes, and the town plat confirms that you've unlawfully trespassed on my land! Indeed, I plan to bring up the very topic at tonight's meeting in town hall—"

"Listen here. you old windbag," he interrupted, shaking a finger. "Either drag me into court or stop flapping your gums day in and day out."

"Well, I never!"

He looked her over from top to toe, his mouth drawing up in the corners. "No, I'll wager you never have."

With a final fierce stare directed his way, Felicity did an abrupt about-face. The watering can slapped against her thigh as she hurried away, dashing up the stone steps to her porch.

With a *thunk*, the screened door shut behind her, though Milton caught her peeking out at him from beyond the gray mesh before her head jerked away.

"Mind your own business, why don't you!" he shouted. Then he spit again, this time directly into her red-berried bushes. Then he undraped himself from the fence.

What a waste of breath that was, he told himself. Not a soul in this town knew how to mind his own business. River Bend was a nesting-ground for busybodies, and damned if they weren't even peskier than sugar ants.

He sighed, stooping to pick up the paper from his weed-choked front walk before tucking it under his arm and heading to the house. For good measure, he let his own screened door slap behind him as he went inside.

His path through the hallway was blocked by a pair of sofa pillows, leftover from a fight with Shotsie the previous night. He kicked them aside.

Flipping on the kitchen light, he found yesterday's coffee and put the pot on the burner to warm. Then he sat down at the table and spread the paper flat. A check of the morning's headlines caused him to abruptly — and loudly — laugh.

"Hey, what's so funny?" Shotsie asked, tugging her sash closed on her robe as she padded into the room. She ran a hand through her mop of yellow curls and yawned, standing behind him. "I could hear you cackling from across the house."

"Those nutty birdwatchers," he said and stabbed a finger at the page. "Just look at that, Shots. Look what those crazy animal huggers are up to now."

NATURE CLUB CALLS LOCAL WHO SOLD LAND TO DEVELOPERS A 'MURDERER,' screamed the bold-faced headline. Below it, the smaller subhead declared, *River Bend's Milton Grone Target of Naturalists.*

"Listen to this garbage," Milton said and bobbed his head as he read. "The pending sale of bluff-side acreage near River Bend has area conservationists up in arms. Not only will countless trees along the Mississippi River be razed to make way for a water park, but wildlife habitat in this unprotected stretch will be threatened as well." He snorted. "What malarkey!" He skimmed several paragraphs before he continued to read aloud. "According to Save the Animal members, Ida Bell and Dorothy Feeny, 'Mr. Grone is no better than a mass murderer. The destruction of woods that provide breeding grounds for eagles and hawks, not to mention more than a dozen other species, is nothing less than genocide. If Milton Grone allows this deal to go through, like the fauna that will die because of his greed, so should he be killed' . . ."

"My, oh, my," Shotsie breathed in his ear.

"Can't those two silly biddies find something better to do than cause me trouble?"

"Milt?"

"Yeah?"

"What's fauna?"

"You think I'm a dictionary or something?" He glared at her. "Go look it up!"

Shotsie pouted but said nothing. Instead, she turned to the stove and poured a cup of coffee. She set the mug on the table before him with such force it slopped over the sides, staining the front page of the paper.

He cursed, but she merely flashed him an innocent smile. Milton tried to ignore her.

"They also called you greedy," she said and pulled a chair up beside him. "Now that's a word I do know."

"So?" He raised an eyebrow.

"So," she prodded. "That must mean you're getting a bundle for that land, huh? You never did tell me how much they settled on giving you anyway."

"That's right," he said, "I didn't."

Shotsie sat still a moment, her wide brown eyes fixed on him, though her silence didn't last long. "Tell me!" she suddenly shrilled at him, her features stained a blotchy pink. "Tell me, I said!" She slapped a fist on the table, shaking it so that Milton's cup of coffee tipped, sending a flood of hot liquid into his lap.

With a yelp, he jumped out of his seat, pulling the thighs of his jeans outward. "You did that on purpose!"

Shotsie stamped the linoleum with a slipper, sticking out her chin. "You never tell me anything, Miltie! Zero! Delilah warned me you were a penny pincher, but I thought it was sour grapes just 'cause of the divorce and all. I mean, at first, you were such a sweetheart, dressing up to take me to the movies and buying me the biggest popcorn with butter. You charmed the pants off me when you smiled. You were so handsome. You promised to love me and take care of me for the rest of my life."

She cocked her head and let out the saddest of sighs. "What happened to *that* Miltie, huh? After living with you for five whole years, I realize your ex was right. This place is a dump." She waved a pudgy hand around. "Everything's ancient and falling apart, and you don't seem to care. We haven't gone to a movie in forever, and you don't even buy me Milk Duds in the checkout line at the supermarket. And now" — she glared — "everyone in town knows you're makin' a bundle off that land you sold, only you won't even tell me the numbers. You're worse than a cheapskate, and I hate you for it!"

Milton ceased dabbing at his wet pants with the kitchen towel and scowled right back at her. "If I'm such a stinker, why don't you shove off and let me be?"

"Maybe I will," Shotsie yelled and, with a sweep of pink slippers and chenille, she turned on her heel and stomped out.

A door slammed up the hallway, and Milton flinched as the house shuddered beneath him. Moments after, he heard Shotsie's overloud sobs through the thin walls.

"Women," he muttered. "Crazier than loons, all of 'em."

His antipathy was deeply ingrained, going back to his mother and her constant nagging. She'd nagged him: *Stand up straight. Keep your elbows off the table. Mind your manners.* She'd nagged his father: *You work too much. You never spend time with your son. You don't help out around the house.*

He still blamed his ma for nagging his pop to the grave, and he'd never forgiven her, even after she'd joined his father in the Grone family plot. Milt's bad first marriage had nearly killed him as well, and now it looked like Shotsie had jumped on the bandwagon.

A pain shot through his chest just then so that, for a full minute after, he struggled hard to catch his breath.

He rubbed at his breastbone, figuring Shotsie would be the death of him yet.

Milton tried to breath deeply as the pain slowly subsided. It was just gas, he told himself, refusing to believe that a tiny ache between his ribs might mean something more. Doc Melville kept telling him his ticker wasn't what it used to be. He'd been after Milt to take those silly nitro pills ever since the pesky bout with his heart that put him in the hospital a while back. But Milton hadn't bought into it. He'd told the doc he felt better than he had in years, that his so-called "heart attack" back when was all his ex-wife's fault and had been quickly remedied by their divorce.

He thumped his chest one last time with the heel of his hand, letting out a far from delicate belch.

Yep. Gas. That's all it was. That and Shotsie.

He glanced at the hallway, through which his wife had disappeared, and he scowled again for good measure.

* * *

It wasn't until nearly seven p.m. that Shotsie emerged from her self-imposed exile. Clad in blue jeans and a sweatshirt advertising a St. Louis beer, she was halfway out the screened door when Milton called to her.

"Where're you off to at this hour?" he shouted from the kitchen. He sat at the table, an oily rag in hand as he cleaned his shotgun. "Don't stay out too long 'cause I'm hungry as a bear, and I don't see dinner on the table."

"Get your own dinner," she shouted back. "I'm going to the town meeting."

"The town meeting," Milton repeated and stopped what he was doing. "What in hell are you doing that for?"

"So the busybodies who know everything can tell me what you're making for killing all those birds and trees up the river!"

He opened his mouth to yell and forbid her to leave. But a tickle of laughter got at him instead, and he howled and hooted at the thought of how the townsfolk would react to seeing her there.

Bang went the door. Her hurried footsteps clomped down the rickety stoop. Through the opened window, he picked up the string of curses she let loose.

His laughter eased to a chuckle, and he wiped the tears from his eyes. Glancing up, he saw darkness snuffing out the last of twilight.

He waited and listened, thinking she'd return and fix him supper. But when several minutes passed and she didn't reappear, Milton gave in to his grumbling stomach and got up to fix himself a sandwich. He ate it there at the table with his cleaned and loaded gun a mere hand's breadth away.

He'd nearly finished his meal when he heard a noise beyond the window, like a critter prowling in the trash. "Damned old woman's cat," he muttered and picked up his shotgun.

Felicity Timmons caused him hell enough without his having to put up with that furry beast of hers making a mess of his garbage.

"Here kitty-kitty," he said in a gruff whisper as he hopped off the stoop and snuck around the house. "C'mon, you darned flea bag, I've got something for you."

He cocked the gun with a clack.

He heard the noise again and hesitated. It sure didn't sound like a cat. It seemed bigger than that. Were those footsteps coming up behind him?

He spun around in time enough to see the shadow that lunged at him, but only that. His gun fell from his hands to the ground, going off as it hit the dirt.

CHAPTER TWO

"Quiet now, please, could I have quiet, everyone?" Art Beaner leaned into the microphone at the podium, sending his nasal tone screeching across the rows of chairs lined up in the small downtown building.

Helen Evans pressed her palms to her ears, waiting until the squeal of Art's voice had died down to nothingness before she peeled them away again.

She looked around her, across the large room used for meetings of the Ladies Civic Improvement League, which she religiously attended; for morning aerobics classes, which she didn't; and Thursdays for town halls. The place had filled up rather quickly. Usually no more than two or three dozen showed up, if that. But this evening's main discussion was a volatile one by River Bend standards, namely the razing of fifty acres up the river in the name of progress. Helen had taken a peek at the plans for the Wet 'n' Woolly Water Park when the board had snagged a copy, and she wasn't any more thrilled than her neighbors at the thought of such pristine land converted to aqua ducts of plastic pipe and slides surrounded by a sea of asphalt.

Helen had lived in this cozy Illinois town for fifty of her seventy-five years, ever since she'd married Joe. She'd borne four children at the hospital in nearby Jerseyville and had reared them in this very spot. Even after that dismal day three years ago when her husband had died, she'd kept up her little house at the corner of Jersey and Springfield. She didn't see the need to change. Some of her best memories had been made there, after all.

Continuity made her feel safe, secure, which was why she enjoyed life in River Bend. There were no McDonald's up the street, no fast-food chains of any sort, just the diner on Main which served a dandy chicken salad and a handful of restaurants over in Grafton. They had little beyond a one-pump gas station that sold bait, an antiques store, a grocery, and a beauty shop. What more, Helen wondered, could one want?

Certainly not a water park, she decided, putting aside her spectacles and the quilting square she'd been stitching. The idea of Milton Grone selling the land to developers tied a knot in her stomach.

"Attention, I said! Attention," Art Beaner called out, this time hammering down the wooden gavel. The motion set the microphone to buzzing angrily again so that a wave of moans erupted and Helen covered her ears again. Until Art tapped the microphone none too gently and got the unnerving noise to stop.

When silence finally reigned, Art cleared his throat and pressed a finger to his horned-rims. "Would, ah, Clara Foley please stand and read the minutes from our last meeting."

From a seat near the front row, a bosomy woman in a purple muumuu rolled to her feet. She flipped open the cover of a steno pad, cocked her grayed head, and began to read: "Meeting commenced with results from the bake sale run by Lola Mueller. We made sixty-five dollars and twenty-three cents to go toward the beautification of Serenity Garden." She paused to lift her double chins. "The peach pie I bought was certainly delicious," she opined.

Helen chuckled as did those around her.

Art Beaner loosened his button-down collar and winced. "To the minutes, Clara, please."

Clara gave him the side-eye before focusing on the dog-eared pages. "Second order of business was the new sewage pump on Springfield. Henry Potter got us a big break with his waste disposal company, which is removing the old pump and installing a new one at a discounted cost." With a skin-wobbling nod, she forged ahead. "The last hour of the meeting was devoted to debate about ways to prevent the construction of Wet 'n' Woolly. Things became so heated and ugly that board chairman Beaner called for the arguments to be postponed until the next Thursday night, which is now," she clarified. "You want me to read the motions?" she asked, staring up at the podium.

Art shook his head.

Flicking her steno pad closed, Clara grinned. "I guess that about covers it," she said and, with a sweep of purple cloth and groan of metal, she sat down to polite applause.

"To continue our discussion of Milton Grone's sale of land to Wet 'n' Woolly," Art began, only to be interrupted by the cry of, "It's an outrage!"

A woman in the front row hopped to her feet. "It's a miscarriage of justice . . . an abomination!" she continued to protest.

Helen smiled at the sight of vocal naturalist Ida Bell in her oversized jodhpurs, shaking a bony fist in the air.

"All those birds . . . the wood owls and thrashers and bobwhites . . . they'll be displaced from their homes," she declared. "The rabbits and deer and squirrels will have to seek refuge in other places." Her angular features flushed with anger, and she shook her head, topped by a tight cap of dark curls. "It makes me sick just to think of it, Mr. Beaner,' she shouted. "Sick, sick, sick!"

"You tell him, Ida!" a small voice yelped, and Helen saw Dotty Feeny pop up from her seat to raise her eager face to her companion.

"I will not allow it to happen," Ida went on, spurred forth by the encouragement. "If I must stop it with my bare hands, I will . . ."

"Miss Bell, please," Chairman Beaner cut in. "I think we all understand your position by now."

"But she's right." Dot stepped up beside her friend, the pair looking every bit like Mutt and Jeff: Ida, tall and thin as a beanstalk, and Dot, short and stocky. "Everything she says is true. It's a sin to let wildlife be destroyed for mere money."

"Speaking of the green stuff . . ."

A voice rose from the rear, and Helen turned — as did the rest of the room — to see who'd spoken.

Helen's breath caught in her throat as Shotsie Grone came forward, tugging at the hem of her yellow sweatshirt, her dark eyes darting this way and that. Helen couldn't recall ever having seen the woman at a town meeting before and wondered what possible motive she had for being there. Surely, she hadn't come to defend her husband's actions?

"I, uh, I'd like to talk a little more about the bucks involved in the deal my, uh, Miltie's gone and made." She raised her dimpled chin while twisting a corkscrew of blond hair around a finger. "The land's not going for cheap, is it? Miltie stands to gain a lot of dough?"

Ida Bell chirped, "You mean you don't know?"

"Well, it's just that I, um . . ." Shotsie faltered, and her chin drooped to her chest. She stopped twirling her hair. Then she looked around the room and her eyes took on a sudden glow. "I'm just wondering how much it would cost if you all were to buy the land from him instead?"

"Us? Pay him?" Ida's tone resounded with skepticism.

The whole room began to whisper, the voices swirling around Helen's ears.

"Why, Mrs. Grone, we don't have that kind of money on hand," Art Beaner said into the crackling microphone. "That would mean millions, and we've barely a fraction of that set aside in our community funds."

"Millions?" Shotsie swayed and pressed a hand between her breasts. "Millions," she repeated though her apparent surprise passed in an instant, and an expression of smugness set in. "Well, then, if you can't match the sale price" — she shrugged — "I guess you'll have to live with the water park. "I'm sure the squirrels will find somewhere else to go."

"Why you silly, little bumpkin!" Ida snorted and started to charge up the aisle only to have Dotty grab hold of her arm, keeping her back.

Shouts erupted from the room's four corners.

Art Beaner pounded his gavel. "Ladies and gentlemen, please," he called out, his forehead glistening beneath the lights. "People of River Bend, get a hold of yourselves and let's discuss this matter rationally!"

"Aw, shut up, Beaner!" someone yelled.

Still, Art continued to plead for silence until the roars turned to grumbles. "Thank you," he said and wiped a sleeve across his brow. "Now if anyone wishes to speak, just raise a hand, I'll point your way, and we'll do this in an orderly fashion."

Helen seemed suddenly to be surrounded by waving arms.

Art stabbed a finger toward Felicity Timmons, seated to Helen's left.

Felicity brushed off her skirt and stood, addressing the chairman in her trilling tone. "I say we should take some action against Mr. Grone. As his neighbor, I've had to put up with his intolerable behavior on a daily basis. He's ignored all standards of common decency. He's made a mockery of the rules. Why, he's built a fence upon my property, and yet he has no intention of removing it! Tell me, Chairman Beaner." Felicity wrung blue-veined hands. "Isn't there something we can do to stop him? Isn't there anyone who can put him in his place?"

"Hey, that's my Miltie you're talking about!" Shotsie cried.

"Mrs. Grone, please," Art said into the whistling microphone.

Helen reached over to take hold of Felicity's trembling hand as her friend slumped to her seat. Helen patted her gently though it didn't do much to erase the other woman's grim expression.

"What about that promise Gerald Grone made before he died?" Henry Potter said, jumping up from his seat. "Didn't he swear he'd leave that land to the town?"

"Henry, I must ask you to wait your turn," Beaner scolded with a wave of the gavel.

"He's right!" Ida Bell stomped to her feet again. "We were all right here in this very room, when Milton's father told us that the acreage would be ours one day. Then he had that dreadful heart attack."

"What about papers?" Shotsie moved further up the aisle, rubbing palms on her thighs. "Did he sign any papers, legal mumbo-jumbo that gave the town Miltie's land?"

Ida stammered, "No, no, but . . ."

"But nothing!" Shotsie's mouth curled triumphantly. "That means Miltie can sell it to anyone he wants and you can't stop him."

"We'll see about that," Ida replied in a most determined tone. Then, with all eyes upon her, she marched through the rows of townsfolk, brushing past Shotsie Grone and heading out of the building altogether.

Like mice drawn by the Pied Piper, the rest of the room followed suit, rising to their feet as they hurried in hot pursuit.

Despite Beaner's pleas for everyone to sit down, the place quickly emptied out.

From her chair, Helen watched the goings-on with concern. Though she knew few River Bend residents were overly fond of Milton Grone — quite the opposite, in fact — none had ever suggested physical violence, despite the fact that most had probably thought of it at one time or another, she was sure.

"Maybe we should do something, Reverend Fister," she said to the man in shirtsleeves seated to her right. "They did sound at the end of their ropes. And you know Mr. Grone. Things could get out of hand if we let them."

"Yes, I know Mr. Grone," the minister remarked quietly and slowly rose from his chair. He hardly appeared a man on a mission. "I know him very well."

"He might need to be saved."

"I think he's past saving," Earnest Fister murmured, the tight frown on his lips drawing a line between peppered mustache and beard.

Helen detected a flicker of aversion in his eyes, and she suspected that the clergyman who conducted services at their tiny chapel every Sunday morning didn't think any more highly of Milton Grone than the rest of the town. Newly-hired the year before, Earnest Fister had moved into a house near the chapel, just a block from the Grones' place. His wife had passed away some time ago, or so Helen had heard, which accounted for him living alone with his teenaged daughter Madeline. Helen couldn't begin to guess what had transpired between the minister and Mr. Grone to make Fister speak of the man with such obvious unease. Though she could certainly believe Milton Grone had done *something* to offend him.

"Shall we go?" she suggested. "I'd hate to see Ida and Dot get into trouble."

"Very well," Fister said and let out a heavy sigh. "If you put it that way, I supposed we must."

With Felicity Timmons and Art Beaner at her heels, Helen left the hall with Fister and headed out. Though the crowd of townsfolk was at least a block ahead, she could hear their upraised voices as they passed picket-fenced yard after yard, striding in the direction of Milton Grone's house like a mob bent on a hanging.

Every now and then through the lamp-lit dark, Helen could make out the arm-waving figure of Shotsie Grone, screaming for them to "Stop it right now, or I'll sue you all!"

Art Beaner followed on Helen's heels, muttering, "Oh, my, oh, my," while to Helen's right, the Reverend Fister plodded ahead in silence.

By the time they turned the corner to the street where Milton Grone lived, Helen saw the several dozen who still followed Ida standing in a semi-circle on the edge of Milton's lawn. Their voices suddenly hushed, and Helen heard no more shouts about bringing Grone to his knees. Instead, there were disquieted murmurs, like things were not as they ought to be, and she found herself suddenly wondering if a shotgun-toting Milton had appeared on his porch.

"Excuse us, please, excuse us," Art Beaner spoke out and managed somehow to break open a path for himself, Helen, Felicity, and Earnest Fister to walk through.

When they emerged at the front of the pack, Helen felt a ripple of anxiety race up her spine.

"Oh, no, oh, no." Shotsie Grone knelt on the ground beside the crumped form of a man, her head shaking. The two appeared fused into a single shadow, hazily lit by the glow of the moon and a distant streetlamp.

"Mrs. Grone?" Helen said and came up behind her.

Shotsie raised her chin and met Helen's gaze. Tears ran down plump cheeks, dripping from eyes turned glassy with shock.

Her movement allowed Helen a glimpse of the man who lay on the unkempt lawn. His skin looked waxy. His eyes stared blankly into the night.

A sob burst from Shotsie's throat, and she uttered something unintelligible, so that Helen couldn't make out a word. But she didn't need to hear. Helen knew precisely what she'd said.

Milton Grone was dead.

CHAPTER THREE

At Helen's urging, several members of the crowd took off for Amos Melville's. The doctor arrived barely five minutes after, his white hair ruffled and brown bag clutched in his hand. He wore a coat thrown over striped pajamas and his feet were stuffed into a pair of loafers.

As gently as she could, Helen pried Shotsie away from her husband. The woman whimpered at first, but then her sobs fast turned into pitiful wails. Helen anchored an arm around Shotsie's trembling shoulders, holding her a safe distance away from Milton's body as Doc Melville got down on hands beside it.

Someone had rounded up flashlights and beamed them down as Amos worked.

Helen looked on with the rest as the doctor shined a pin light into Milton's unseeing pupils, touched his fingers to the man's throat, and then lifted a lifeless hand upward to check fingernails for color.

After a quick listen with his stethoscope, Doc Melville stuffed it back into his bag. "The light, please, shine it here," he said before he rolled Milton's head toward him, clucking aloud as he scrutinized the side of the skull that had rested upon an uprooted stone.

He sighed as he gently lowered the Milton's head to the position in which he'd found it. Without a word, he closed his leather satchel and rose from his knees, brushing dirt from his pajamas as he faced Milton's wife.

Helen tightened her arm around Shotsie as Amos Melville cleared his throat, pressing at the bridge of his spectacles.

"I'm sorry, Mrs. Grone," he began, "but I warned Milton many times to take better care of himself. His heart wasn't what it used to be, despite how robust he appeared. If only he'd been more serious about his condition. If only he'd taken his nitroglycerine as I prescribed. Well, perhaps, we might have prolonged his life by a few more years."

Shotsie's teary eyes widened. "What exactly are you saying, Doc? What's this 'condition' you mentioned? You don't mean his hemorrhoids?"

Before the doctor replied, he met Helen's eyes. He looked as puzzled as she. "You didn't know about Milton's myocardial infarction ten years back?"

"His myo . . . what?" Shotsie shook her head. "I don't understand."

"He had a massive heart attack," Doc explained to Shotsie's gasp. "I was your husband's physician for more years than I'd like to recall, and he was as stubborn as an ox every one of them. His heart problems were his Achille's heel. I guess he didn't want to trouble you about it, what with you being younger than he was."

"A heart attack," she murmured.

"He was in the hospital for nearly a month," Amos told her. "I must say that, for a time, we were afraid he wasn't going to make it. But his orneriness pulled him through all right."

Shotsie pulled away from Helen and looked at the people who still milled about as if searching for someone. She hesitated before pointing a finger at Ida Bell. "This one here said Miltie's father died of a heart attack. Is that true?"

Doc nodded. "It seems a good many diseases involving the heart are inherited."

“So that’s what happened to Miltie?”

Again, Amos nodded. “From the looks of things, I’d say yes. Though there is a rather nasty gash on his head where he struck that rock when he fell. I’d like to examine him further.” He paused to wave around them, at the dark and the people who hovered about. “But in better equipped surroundings.”

“A heart attack,” Shotsie repeated, seeming to have a hard time digesting the news.

Helen reached out, but then withdrew her hand, not wanting to intrude. So, it startled her when Shotsie released a hysterical sob and threw herself on the ground beside Milton, pressing her cheek to his chest. Her hands clutched at his shoulders. “Oh, Miltie, why now? Why now when you just got all that water-park money?”

Helen looked at Amos, and he shook his head.

“Stand back, everyone,” Art Beaner piped up. “The sheriff’s arrived.”

The folks who remained on Milton Grone’s lawn backed off as the town’s only squad car pulled up without the benefit of lights or siren. It parked in front of the battered mailbox with the peeling G sticker.

Sheriff Frank Biddle slid out from behind the wheel, wearing in mud-splattered boots and rumpled uniform. He’d donned his holster which hung precariously beneath a good-sized belly. As he approached Helen and Doc, he tipped his hat and puffed up his chest like a peacock.

“Got a call from Henry Potter,” he said. “He mentioned there was trouble at the Grones.” He glanced in Shotsie’s direction, and his eyes narrowed. He otherwise seemed unperturbed by the scene. “What’s up, Doc? Did old Milt finally go boots up and leave us all in peace?”

“Sheriff, really!” Helen frowned at him, jerking her chin toward the still-sobbing Shotsie.

“Sorry, ma’am,” he said quickly and turned around, checking out the handful of townsfolk still hanging about.

Helen saw the tail of his blue pajama top sticking out in back where he’d missed tucking it into his trousers.

"Got a cause of death, Doc?" he asked.

"Looks like a heart attack," Amos replied.

"His heart? I didn't know he had one," the sheriff quipped, though his grin quickly vanished when Helen fixed her eyes upon him.

Doc nodded. "I'd like to examine the body, Sheriff, so if we could get an ambulance here to move him."

"No problem."

"Um, Sheriff." Art Beaner emerged from the shadows behind Helen. He held a shotgun awkwardly in his hands. "I found this sticking out of the bushes not far from the bod . . . from Mr. Grone."

Biddle took the gun and raised the barrel to his nose. He sniffed then tapped the butt. "It's been fired recently. Still smells of burned powder."

The acrid odor was faint but Helen could smell it as well. "Perhaps Mr. Grone himself fired it," she suggested. "Everyone in town knew he kept the thing loaded. Maybe he heard something that brought him outside."

"Like a squirrel in his trash, or Miss Timmons' cat," Art mentioned, running a hand over thinning hair. "As a matter of fact, Felicity told me he took a shot at Kitty just a week ago. Scared Felicity to death."

"Not as much as the cat, I'll wager," the sheriff said, though no one laughed.

"He could have fired at an animal then dropped the gun when his heart gave out," Art suggested. "You think that might be the case, Doc?"

"I can't be sure of anything until I've had a chance to properly look at the body," Amos said. "If you'll get that ambulance here, Sheriff, we can proceed straightaway."

"Gotcha, Doc."

The sheriff headed over to his black and white, and Helen heard the crackle of static from his radio as he called for an ambulance.

Helen helped Doc separate Shotsie from Milton, a task that was harder than anticipated. It took some persistent pleading before Shotsie allowed Helen to move her aside so that Doc and the Sheriff could prepare Milton's body for transport.

Ida Bell and Dot Feeny took that moment to approach the grieving widow as she wept in Helen's arms.

At Dotty's nudge, Ida asked, "If there's anything we might do to help, Mrs. Grone . . ."

"Help?" Shotsie stiffened, jerking out of Helen's grasp. She sucked in a breath before lifting her chin and hissing at the pair, "I don't want anything from either of you. Nothing! As I see it, you as good as killed my Miltie. Because of all the trouble you caused him with your stupid threats, he's gone and left me, you understand? And he's not coming back!"

Ida and Dot looked stunned to silence.

Helen couldn't blame them.

Shotsie squared her shoulders, wiped the tears from her cheeks with dirt-smeared fingers, then strode toward the house. The screened door banged shut loudly behind her.

Up to that moment, Earnest Fister had kept quiet vigil by the fence. He picked his way across the yard with its uprooted rocks and knee-high weeds, stopping near Helen, Ida, and Dot only long enough to announce, "I think this is where I come in. I'll go talk to Mrs. Grone and try to calm her down."

Dotty clasped bird-like hands between her ample breasts and moaned, "What a horrible thing. Simply awful."

Helen patted her arm. "Yes, yes, it is. Death is never easy."

"Oh, no." Dot turned her plump face to Helen. "I meant what Mrs. Grone just said, that Ida and I are to blame for Milton's passing. That simply wasn't at all kind."

"She's upset, Dot," Helen reminded. "She's had a terrible shock."

"I don't think anyone's sorry that he's gone," Ida remarked in her overloud way. "I don't mean to be crass, but he wasn't the most human of beings. He treated us all like pebbles in his shoes. Without him around, life in this town will improve immensely."

"Ida, for goodness' sake!" Helen couldn't believe what she'd heard. It wasn't like Ida to be so callous, most certainly not at a moment like this.

Ida crossed her thin arms over her chest and set her booted feet apart. "I can't help it, Helen. He was just plain no good. Though I'm concerned for all living creatures on our planet, I hardly had a soft spot in my heart for Milton Grone. All he's done ever since his father died is stir up trouble. He used to just ignore what went on in town, but losing his dad turned him bitter and mean. He's made Felicity a nervous wreck, the poor thing. Now she's free of him, isn't she?"

"Yes, now she's free," Dot echoed.

Helen searched around them, having not seen Felicity since they'd reached Milton's property. She finally spotted her across the split-rail fence, standing in her own yard, silhouetted quite clearly by her porch light.

She watched as Felicity went toward a cluster of bushes and stooped to retrieve a pair of gloves from the ground. She pressed them into the large pockets of her duster.

Then Felicity bent again, this time to grab the long handle of a shovel. She took it with her back to the house and leaned it against the porch before she disappeared inside.

"Dear Felicity," Helen murmured, unable to refute either Ida's or Dot's remarks about Milton's death somehow freeing her.

But then, Helen knew, Felicity would not be the only one breathing a sigh of relief now that Milton Grone was gone.

CHAPTER FOUR

Earnest Fister sat at his desk in the small office at the rear of the chapel, staring down at a blank sheet of paper. He pressed the tip of his pen on the page, but his mind couldn't focus. His heart was too heavy.

Writer's block rarely happened to him. He'd always loved the written word. It had drawn him to the ministry in the first place. Earnest usually took great pleasure in creating sermons, describing events from his own life and drawing on pertinent Biblical passages to underscore the message he wanted to share.

On this particular day, however, he found putting pen to paper less a joy than a form of torture.

He needed something for Milton Grone's funeral service to be held the following day. Yet every pithy expression that came to mind at times like this, every hopeful and inspiring sentence about the dearly departed as a loving father or doting husband, as a devote churchgoer and town citizen, all rang false. For him to portray Milton Grone in such a way was akin to deceit. And should he utter those flowery phrases tomorrow, every soul in River Bend would know it as well as he.

So how might he describe the person Milton Grone was in life without speaking ill of the dead?

Fister sighed, setting down his pen. For a long moment, he rubbed his beard, unsure of where to go from here. He finally got up and walked toward the sole window to grace the study behind the apse. Made of two divided panes of stained glass, the window was the room's centerpiece. A simple bronze plaque beneath read: Donated by Gerald and Eda Grone. Milton's father and mother, or so he'd been told.

Earnest unhooked the latch that united the colorful scene of the Virgin Mary and baby Jesus, and he pushed the window open so the afternoon breeze could stir his thoughts.

The whir of a lawn mower hummed through the air, and he imagined he could smell the fresh-cut grass. Children's voices rang out from a nearby playground: happy sounds of laughter, strains of "Ring Around the Rosey," and the faint squeal of the swings as tiny legs pumped them to and fro.

A smile tugged at his lips, the childish noises striking a near-forgotten chord somewhere inside him. He remembered when his own daughter Maddy was so young as that; when he'd taken her to the park, caught her at the bottom of the slide and swung her around in his arms before her feet touched ground again.

His mouth tightened suddenly, becoming a thin line that he wore often now.

Had he done all he could for her? Had he done his best? It had been so difficult being both father and mother to the girl ever since his Margaret had died when Maddy was barely eleven. He'd wanted to do what was right for her always; perhaps, he'd been too strict and not because of his profession, but because he'd been afraid. He'd had to counsel so many adolescents at his old church in St. Louis, children barely into their teens who were hooked on drugs or booze; girls younger than Madeline who'd found themselves pregnant.

He'd never wanted those things for Maddy. He'd tried to keep her safe. He'd hoped it would be different for them here in this quiet town of River Bend, set so snugly between the bluffs of the Mississippi. He'd prayed it would bring them closer again somehow. Instead, his being so overprotective had only pushed her away.

"Please, Maddy, talk to me," he'd begged her in recent days. "Can you just tell me what you're thinking? What do you want from me? Tell me how to make things right."

"I'm nearly eighteen, Daddy," she'd told him, looking a decade past in her tiny shorts and cut-off sweatshirt. Her dainty features looked garish beneath excessive make-up in too-bright hues. She'd given a toss to her shiny dark hair as she'd finished, "It's too late for you to start fixing things."

Fixing things?

When, Earnest wondered, had they been broken? And who had done the breaking?

He pulled the pair of panes closed, latching them tightly and shutting out the carefree noises of the playground which suddenly seemed so unfriendly.

He turned away from the stained glass, his gaze settling on his unwritten eulogy for Milton Grone. He had to come up with something, but what was there to say? God help him, but he felt no remorse at the man's death. It was his duty to look for something good — any tiny, little thing — in everyone he met. But after being Milton's neighbor this past year, he'd come up empty. The truth was that Mr. Grone had not been a kind man, nor had he been generous in any way, though Fister had not given up on him completely, not at first.

Earnest had tried to encourage him to attend the Sunday services, to join their Bible study, to simply search deep inside for whatever gift God had dealt him. But Milton had wanted no part of any of it.

"Why should I?" he'd asked. "What's God ever done for me, or the church for that matter? I don't need salvation if that's where you're going with this. All those fancy speeches you make . . . they're just a lot of gobbledygook to me. Real pretty, maybe, but they don't amount to much of anything. Besides, your pretty words haven't seemed to help the God-fearing people of this town much. If anyone needs saving, it's them. Biggest bunch of hypocrites I've ever seen."

Milton had shown an interest in one aspect of Fister's life, however: teenaged Maddy.

"She's a good-looking girl, preacher," Grone had told him flat-out. "Better keep your eye on her or someone's gonna pluck her right from under your nose."

Earnest recalled the look in Grone's eyes, the sly smile on his lips, and his hands tightened to fists at the memory.

No. He couldn't say he'd miss Milton Grone. In fact, what he felt, if not gladness, was a sense of relief.

Though the truth in this instance was something he had to work his way around gently, or he'd have nothing to say at the funeral tomorrow. Nothing, save for "Amen."

CHAPTER FIVE

Helen Evans stood behind the porch screen, refusing to open the door to the twenty-pound yellow tomcat who sat just outside, the remains of a field mouse dangling from his jaws.

"I'm sorry, Amber," she said, "but you're not coming in with that thing in your mouth. Go on then. Shoo. Have your snack somewhere else and come back when you've finished."

The cat stared at her for the longest time, as if debating whether to go or stay. Then with an irritated swish of his tail, he popped onto his large paws and descended the stoop, the dead mouse swinging like a rubber toy.

Helen shook her head as she watched him go, thinking that having a cat was much like coexisting with a very independent child: in the end, like the child, the cat often seemed to get his way. Except when there was a rodent involved, she decided, shuddering.

She checked her wristwatch.

Twenty to noon.

She'd better get a move on if she wanted to make it to Lola Mueller's on time for her luncheon date with the girls. "The girls" being about a dozen other ladies of River Bend who were members of their weekly Stitch and Sew, more commonly referred to as "Stitch and Bitch" since there was, admittedly, a good deal more gossip that went on than actual needlework.

In fifteen minutes, she was out of her sweatsuit and properly attired in blouse and skirt. She even managed to tame her wiry gray hair into an acceptable style. She dabbed on a touch of pink lipstick before she snatched up her quilting bag and headed out the door.

Clara Foley lumbered by just then, heading in the same direction. After breezy "hellos," Helen fell into step with her. A few minutes after, they reached Lola's place. The porch buzzed with vociferous chatter, and Helen was reminded of the noisy banter of caged birds in the pet store.

"Helen! Clara! Come right on in," Lola's mellifluous voice called out from behind the porch screens. "You're the very ones we've been waiting for."

Clara went inside first, her pink muumuu billowing with a gust of wind. Helen entered after, acknowledging greetings sent her way by those already gathered on their wicker perches.

Ida Bell and Dorothy Feeny sat side by side on a wooden swing bolted to the beamed ceiling. The two looked uncomfortable as always, out of place anywhere, Helen imagined, but their Save the Animal meetings. They attended Stitch and Sew under duress from their friends and, Helen decided, doubtless with hopes that one day their remarks about the demise of this species or that would send the less political women into action.

Clara positioned herself on the cushioned divan, squeezing in between Gladys Potter, wife of Henry of waste disposal fame, and Sarah Biddle, the better half of their local sheriff.

Doc Melville's wife Fanny nodded from a rocking chair. Her knitting lay neatly in her lap, the needles madly clicking.

Felicity Timmons sat primly nearby. Her cotton shirt was polka-dotted with water marks. Her green sneakers had faint slashes of dirt on the toes.

The poor dear looked tired, Helen thought. There were shadows beneath the pale blue of her eyes, and the lines on her face looked deeper. Rouge lent color to her wrinkled cheeks. Otherwise, her skin was white as snow, protected from the sun by her ever-present hats. Today, she'd donned a familiar white straw number tied with a vivid green bow. Beneath its wide brim, Felicity's chin tipped down, her face nearly hidden. Her hands trembled as she raised her coffee cup and sipped.

The events of the previous night had certainly shaken the woman and understandably so. Milton Grone might have been a real thorn in Felicity's side, but he *had* been her neighbor. Seeing him lying dead just beyond the fence could not have been easy to stomach, not for one as sensitive as Felicity.

"Hello," Helen said to her friend, smiling as she took the empty chair beside her. "How are you holding up?"

Coffee slopped over the sides of the cup as Felicity returned it to its saucer. "Fine," she got out. "And why shouldn't I be?"

"What with Milton's death and all," Helen started to say before pausing, detecting a flicker of fear in Felicity's eyes at the mention — a tightening of her frown — and she let the words hang.

Though the subject took but seconds for another to broach.

"Can you believe it, girls?" Clara Foley said, patting her knees. "Can you truly believe that old Grinch has finally breathed his last? I, for one, thought we'd never live to see the day. You know how they say that only the good die young. The mean ones last forever!"

A few chuckled, while others clucked.

Helen didn't join in their laughter. Her gazed was on Felicity, who seemed to shrink beneath her hat brim.

"Let's talk about something else, shall we?" she suggested and brightly turned to the others. "Like the upcoming Founder's Day picnic?"

"The picnic? Pah!" Gladys Potter harrumphed. Framed by white curls, her long face frowned at Helen, as if Helen were a spoilsport trying to ruin all their fun. "Not when we've got Milton Grone's death to discuss. Why it's the buzz of the town."

"She's right, it is," Sarah Biddle said, her overbite giving her a horsey appearance. "I was at the post office this morning, and everyone there was blathering on about it. I mean, wasn't it such a shock?"

"What does Amos say, Fanny?" Clara asked. "I heard he's got Milton's body under a microscope. Has he found something fishy?"

The click-clack of knitting needles ceased, and Doc Melville's wife looked up, spectacles low on her nose. "I'm sure the doctor will let everyone know in due time if his exam turns up anything. But, for now, it seems Mr. Grone passed from a heart attack. I can't imagine why you all find it so darned interesting."

"Goodness, Fanny, but you're a killjoy," Lola Mueller chided as she walked around with a pot of coffee, freshening empty cups. "We're just curious."

Fanny sighed and resumed her knitting. "All Amos told me was that he wanted to check out that gash on Grone's head. He can only do so much on his own though. If there's any more to it, he'll have to send the body over to his friend at the medical examiner's office."

"I'm sure it won't come to that since it was surely a heart attack," Ida said dully. She and Dotty moved the swing gently to and fro with their toes. "Can't we please get off this silly topic and onto one that matters, like the impending extinction of the red-spotted blue bills . . ."

"What the devil are those?" Clara asked, rolling her eyes. "Some kind of bug?"

Ida's face flushed, and she set the heels of her boots flat on the floor, bringing the swing to a sudden stop. Dot's squat form, lower in gravity, pitched forward so that she would have fallen off if not for Ida's outstretched arm.

"They are not insects!" Ida announced, puffing out her thin chest. "They are a most rare duck, sent over from China during the Ming Dynasty by the Emperor himself!"

Clara opened wide her generous mouth and patted it with her palm.

Ida crossed her arms snugly and glared.

"Girls, please, stop this," Lola said with a clap of her hands. Her small eyes squinted as she frowned. "Let's not waste our hour together by arguing about ducks."

"No, let's get back to Milton Grone kicking the bucket," Sarah Biddle insisted. "My Frank said Grone's wife — I mean, his widow — threw herself on the body and cried hysterically."

"Well, wouldn't you be hysterical if something happened to the sheriff?" Gladys Potter asked.

Sarah's rabbit teeth caught her bottom lip as she smiled. "Goodness, Gladys, can't I have a minute to think about it?"

Clara burst into loud guffaws, slapping her thighs with relish. The others laughed politely, save for Felicity who'd not made a sound.

"I think I need some air," she murmured, setting down cup and saucer with a clatter. She quickly rose to her feet and, with a terse goodbye to their hostess, went through the door and out. Her shoes crunched on the graveled road as she hurried off, the ribbon from her hat trailing behind her like a streamer.

Helen thought about packing up the quilt square she'd been half-heartedly working on and pursuing her friend. But Felicity's quick stride assured her that the old girl didn't want company. She needed time to herself.

"Tsk, tsk." From across the porch, Gladys Potter clicked tongue against teeth, causing Helen to look over. "I think this whole episode with Milton Grone has affected dear Felicity more deeply than the rest of us."

"Well, she does — or rather, she did — live next door to the man," Ida remarked, her thin neck arched like an underfed swan's. "If you'd had to put up with that bear in such close proximity, you'd probably feel as guilty as she does."

"Guilty?" Helen scoffed, pricked by the insinuation. "Why in heaven should she? Felicity didn't kill him."

"Perhaps not," Ida responded. "But I'll bet she's wished him dead at least a thousand times. I know I did, and I'm sure I'm not alone. I doubt there's a citizen in this town who didn't have a run-in with Milton that left them wishing he'd go away for good. And if they denied it, they'd be lying."

The declaration brought down an uncomfortable silence so that even the garrulous Clara was temporarily without rebuttal.

"Cake, anyone?" Lola offered, finally breaking up the unfamiliar hush.

This time, Clara was not so slow to reply. "Wonderful idea," she said. "I'll help you cut."

No more was spoken about Milton Grone at the gathering.

Still, Helen left Lola's thinking about what Ida had said, that Milton Grone had made his share of enemies in River Bend. As she let herself into her own house, Amber on her heels — this time, without the mouse — Helen found herself counting all those who'd despised Milton Grone enough to kill him, and she felt a rush of relief that he'd died of cardiac arrest.

Otherwise, one of River Bend's own might end up in handcuffs.

CHAPTER SIX

Amos Melville squinted at the slide of human tissue through his high-powered microscope, not pleased at all with what he saw.

He lifted his head, moving away from the eyepiece, instead gazing down at the open folder near his elbow. Though the pages were already filled with his scribbles, he picked up his pen and added further notes. He wrote quickly, wanting to capture his thoughts while they were fresh in his mind, before the flow was broken.

He'd examined Milton Grone as thoroughly as his own little lab would allow, taking x-rays and tissue samples from the wound on Milton's skull.

And he didn't like the results. No, he didn't like them at all.

He called on Ed Drake, an old college chum and a medical examiner for the county, and he relayed his concerns. Within a half hour, Drake had shown up in River Bend to talk with Amos face to face. Then he left with the body, promising to do a few lab tests in-house and then deliver Milton to the local mortuary in time for the funeral the following day.

Doc prayed that Ed Drake wouldn't find anything that changed the initial finding of "cardiac arrest" as the cause of death on the death certificate. But a sense of doubt nagged at him.

A thatch of white hair fell upon his furrowed brow, but he didn't raise a hand to push it off. "Lord above, but I hope my suspicions are wrong," he muttered, knowing if he wasn't, the good people of River Bend would surely have something juicy to gossip about, something much more disquieting than a catty remark whispered by one gray-haired matron to another over a hand of bridge. No, it would be far worse.

If Doc was right in his assumption, it could mean that someone in town was a killer.

CHAPTER SEVEN

Felicity Timmons approached the yard of her well-kept Victorian house, pausing at the gate opened wide to the inlaid brick walkway.

She looked to her left, eyeing the fence that trespassed on her land by half a foot. Then she surveyed the property beyond the split rails: the weed-invested grounds and paint-peeled home set on concrete slabs veined with cracks.

Instinctively, she searched for the man with the sunburned face and untamed hair, clad in undershirt and well-worn denim. But she saw no one there, merely a vacant window staring back at her, its shade partially drawn like a half-closed eyelid.

There was no rusted lawn mower running unattended, its noisy motor enough to inspire a migraine. No one sloppily sprayed herbicide about so that it rained down fatally upon the raspberry bushes. No slouched figure hung over the fence, smirking at her and taunting her with remarks that made her blush.

She let out a held breath, her heartbeat easing as her blood pressure came down. Grone was dead, she reminded herself, and he wasn't coming back.

She fairly swayed with relief at the thought.

Felicity had never liked Milton Grone, not one little bit. She'd always believed he'd get his just desserts sooner or later. She was just sorry that it hadn't been sooner.

With a sniff, she went around to the rear of the house, touching a camellia bud along the way, cooing softly to a droopy rhododendron. They were her children, these plants, and she cared for them as such. She'd never been married — engaged once, yes, till her fiancé got cold feet — though she hadn't dwelled on it overmuch. She had worked for the British railway for half of her life, selling tickets to people traveling here and there while she'd gone nowhere. And finally, she'd up and quit, using her savings to travel before it was too late, viewing scenery that inspired her senses and her green thumb beyond the roses of her native England: the tulips in Holland, the rain forests of Costa Rica, the gardens of Versailles, and the verdant vineyards of Tuscany. Then Felicity had jumped the pond to take a river boat cruise down the Mississippi one fall, and she'd been smitten by what she'd seen. Once she'd glimpsed the winding river edged by craggy bluffs painted amazing shades of gold, red, and yellow — witnessed her first bald eagle in flight and thought, "that is me!" — she fell in love with the beauty and simplicity of the region and decided to remain.

Since she'd settled in tiny River Bend all those years ago, she'd been happy as a clam, gardening each day, puttering about in the dirt, and taking walks up to the river's edge to listen to the brown waters lapping gently upon the rocky shore.

The only thing had had marred her peaceful existence was Milton Grone, as ungrateful a fellow as she'd ever known. His parents had once lived in the house next door. Gerald and Eda had been all that Milt was not: polite, thoughtful, generous. Though hardly a rich man by the standards of the day, Gerald had given what he could to the township, more in deeds than in dollars. Eda had been a tough bird, trying to support her husband's endeavors and raise a son who seemed to have little respect for her or for anyone else. When Gerald and Eda had passed, they'd willed their money to River Bend. It had been barely enough to restore the old lighthouse and build a new playground, but more than enough to irritate his son, bringing him home again.

Felicity settled into a wrought iron chair on her back patio, remembering all the dust Milton had kicked up when he'd returned with his then-wife Delilah. They hadn't been satisfied with receiving Gerald and Eda's house and the quarter acre it sat on. They'd scoffed when they'd learned that there was no financial windfall; that other than the old homestead all Milton had inherited was undeveloped acreage up the river.

"What in the hell am I gonna do with a bunch of trees?" Milton had yelled loudly enough for all the neighbors to hear. "What good will they do me?"

He'd tried to sell the plot to the town as he'd wanted it off his hands. But the town council had declined. Milton had wanted an exorbitant amount for it, more than River Bend's coffers could pay. Milton only had to wait a decade or so for Wet 'n' Woolly to step in.

Felicity shook her head. Why hadn't Gerald bequeathed the land to the town as he'd promised? What had made him change his mind, she wondered, or had he? But there was no documentation to back up that promise, none that anyone could find.

The only aspect of it all that made Felicity feel in the least bit better was in knowing that Milton Grone had died before he could enjoy his jackpot.

"Enough of this," she said and patted her thighs. "Pull yourself up by your bootstraps, old girl," she admonished and, with a push, did arise.

She pulled on her soiled gloves and looked around for her trowels. Where had she put them? And where was her shovel?

Ah, yes! During the to-do the previous night, she'd set them near the porch. She hadn't cleaned them and put them away as she should have. She'd been so flustered, what with

Milton pestering her earlier in the day. And then came the town meeting and the fuss of finding the body. It's a wonder she hadn't forgotten about her tools altogether.

The shovel leaned against the lattice. The tip of the spade stuck in the dirt. The trowels lay scattered thereabouts. She wouldn't need the shovel anyway, she realized, and left it where it was, deciding to wash it off later when she had finished up her other tasks.

She'd purchased a lovely flat of marigolds a few days before, and they waited patiently in plastic pots on her porch steps. The trowels would do just fine, she decided, picking them up before retrieving the flowers.

Once she'd deposited everything beside the empty plot near the gate, she began to dig, whistling as she rooted each marigold in the fertilized loam. "You're safe now," she told them as she toiled. "You're safe, you see, because that bloody awful man is gone. Very soon he'll either be ashes or buried," she assured them, "put under the earth deeper than any of you, never to be uprooted."

A cloud washed over the sun for a moment, banishing the warmth that had touched her shoulders and back. The sudden chill made the hairs on her neck stand on end, and Felicity stood, looking over and across the fence, her breath catching in her throat.

Had the window shade at the Grones' house come up just a bit? Had someone stood there, watching her a minute before?

A shiver raced up her spine.

The sun reappeared, warming her back, and Felicity shook off her apprehension. Milton was dead, she reminded herself. He couldn't bother her any more.

She patted the ground around the frilly leaves of her marigolds, noting the sunward tilt of their golden heads, and she smiled.

CHAPTER EIGHT

Still clad in the skirt and blouse she'd worn to Stitch and Sew, Helen finished putting plastic wrap around the zucchini bread she'd baked that morning and headed out of the house to pay a call on Shotsie Grone.

When she reached their street, she saw Felicity in her yard, planting annuals, and Helen stopped just long enough to ask after her. Her friend did appear less preoccupied than she'd been at Lola Mueller's. But Felicity had always found solace in the earth.

Helen moved on to the house next door, pausing at the dented mailbox before forging ahead on the cracked sidewalk toward the Grones' front porch.

"Hello?" she called through the screen of the door. "Anyone home?"

"Come on in," a voice shouted with more impatience than welcome. "I'm in the kitchen!"

Helen went inside, leaving the sunshine and entering a narrow hallway devoid of light save for what filtered in through a grime-covered window.

She and Joe had been here to dinner often when Eda and Gerald were alive, though it had been quite a while since. The place had been kept up far better then, the paint fresh, the floors swept, and sills dusted. Still, in spite of the changes, she knew her way around well enough to find the kitchen.

"Mrs. Grone?" she said as she made her way past faded wallpaper toward Shotsie's voice. She paused in the doorway, cradling the plastic-wrapped bread in her arms, finding herself at a loss for words.

Dead ahead at a litter-strewn table sat the newly-widowed Mrs. Grone, wrapped in a shapeless bathrobe. The head topped by corkscrew curls drooped so that chin sat on chest. Shotsie clutched a box of tissues with one hand. The other held a single filmy sheet into which she abruptly — and loudly — blew her nose.

"Am I interrupting?" Helen asked, taking a tentative step forward. "I could always come back—"

"No, no." Shotsie waved the used tissue overhead like a flag of surrender. "It's all right."

Helen wasn't so sure. She knew how it felt to lose a husband and, though she would hardly compare Milton Grone to her Joe, she understood how Shotsie must hurt.

"I brought you zucchini bread," she said, feeling rather silly offering the food, as it was hardly a cure for grief. "I'll put it on the counter if you'd like."

"Whatever." Shotsie loudly sighed.

Helen could see the toll her tears had taken. She looked so different from the woman who'd burst into town hall the night before. Her face was devoid of make-up, pale and childlike. Shadows of gray ringed her eyes beneath the sag of her uncombed curls.

"You poor dear," Helen said and went to her side, setting the bread amid the clouds of tissue on the table, taking Shotsie's cold hand into her own. "What can I do for you?" she asked. "This must be so difficult, I know."

"Do you?" Shotsie jerked out of her grasp. She sniffled, eyeing Helen skeptically. "Do you really?"

"Of course, I do." Helen set her hands in her lap.

A smile tugged at Shotsie's mouth. "You sound like everyone else in this town." She dabbed roughly at her eyes and laughed angrily. "All those do-gooders who never welcomed me when I married Milton."

"They only want to help," Helen said.

Shotsie blew her nose again. "You mean they only want to ease their guilty conscience. Everyone despised Miltie. I would've had to be deaf, dumb, and blind not to see. Since the day Milt moved me in, hardly anyone's ever said 'boo' to me. And during this whole thing with Wet 'n' Woolly, there was all that name-calling and threats." She shook her head. "You'd have thought Miltie murdered someone the way we were treated. He would've had to be a saint to put up with what he did."

Helen shifted in her seat, thinking that Milton Grone was hardly Mother Teresa. She didn't know quite what to say, which was probably just as well. Shotsie wasn't finished.

"No one gave a damn about him when he was alive so why should I believe they care now that he's dead? Unless they assume the land deal will fall through with him gone." Shotsie pushed a hand through her limp curls. "Well, they'll find out soon enough that I'm not breaking off Miltie's deal with those developer fellows. Nothing's changing where that's concerned. Milt wanted that land sold to the water park, and I'll make sure it all goes through just like he planned, even if it's the last thing I do. You got that, Mrs. Evans?"

"I do," Helen said. Then she cleared her throat, steering the conversation into even muddier waters. "I was wondering, if you've called Delilah—"

"Delilah?" Shotsie stiffened. "Why should I?"

Helen smoothed her skirt, wondering if perhaps she'd have been better off not broaching the subject at all. "She was married to Milton."

"A hundred years ago!"

"They do have two children."

"They're ungrateful brats," Shotsie said and sounded like she was choking. "Miltie hadn't seen them forever. They never even sent him a Father's Day card."

Helen watched the play of emotions on Shotsie's face, seeing the mix of uncertainty and disgust. She didn't doubt that there was little love lost between the two Mrs. Grones. But fair was fair. "They should be told Milton's dead regardless," she insisted. "He was their father after all."

Shotsie's frown deepened. "You know what's gonna happen then, don't you? They're going to want a piece of the water park deal. No way," she said and vigorously shook her head. "No way are they going to see so much as a penny. Not after what they're nasty mother put Miltie through. Did you know she'd threatened to sic a lawyer on him for back child support? Oh, and unpaid alimony, too, even though he swore she'd gotten more than enough."

"No," Helen said, and she wasn't sure that was any of her business. "I'm sorry, no, I didn't."

Shotsie toyed with the tissue in her hands and sniffed. "Milton mostly kept his problems to himself," she whispered, "and so did I."

Helen attempted a smile. "Maybe now, because of this, you'll come out of the house more often and give us all a chance to get to know you better, and you to know us."

Shotsie shifted her gaze, staring at Helen. "You've gotta be joking, right? 'Cause I'll tell you something, Mrs. Evans, just as soon as I've taken care of things here, I'm clearing out. With Miltie gone, there's nothing to keep me in this dump a minute longer."

"You should give the town a chance," Helen tried to say, but Shotsie sharply cut her off.

"A chance?" she repeated, her cheeks blotched pink. "You figure I'll get cozy with that Felicity Timmons next door, huh? She's a real pal, that one. She'd like me better if I were a petunia. I can see her from the window, playing in the dirt every day from sunup to sundown." Shotsie snorted. "That old bag was nothing but snooty to Milt and me, always complaining about this or that. Like the fence Miltie built. He worked hard on it, too, pullin' up rocks the size of cannonballs so he could put in the posts." Her fingers plucked at the tissue, shredding it to strips. "No, I don't doubt Felicity's kicking up her sensible heels now that Milt's dead. And those two birdbrains from that nature club, I'll bet they're celebrating, too."

Helen noted the feverish glint in Shotsie's eyes, and she figured it was time to skedaddle. She came to her feet, the chair screeching on the uneven linoleum as she pushed her way out. "You should lie down," she told Shotsie. "You must be tired after everything."

Shotsie opened her mouth as though to object then closed it promptly, her lips vaguely quivering. As suddenly, she broke into sobs, her shoulders sinking as tears spilled from her eyes. Her wails echoed through the house.

"Oh, my," Helen breathed and her mothering instincts kicked in. She gently guided Shotsie from the table, tucking the smaller woman to her side. "Come along and let's get you tucked into bed. Then I'll leave you alone so you can sleep."

Helen led the crying widow to a room at the back of the house, settling her in bed, just as she'd promised. She slipped out a few minutes after, hurrying toward home and wondering all the while if Shotsie would make it through the funeral the next day without falling apart; knowing it was going to be difficult enough for everyone as it was.

CHAPTER NINE

Shotsie scowled as she stared down at the black dress laid out across the bed. It was as plain and drab as the Wal-Mart underpants Milt had bought her. No lace, no baubles, no frills.

She sighed, hardly able to imagine anything drearier.

Reluctantly, she snatched up the dress and stepped into it. She had to shimmy to pull it past her thighs and over her half-slip. The shiny polyester briefly snagged on her safety-pinned brassiere before she could twist to zip it up. When she was done and panting lightly at the exertion, she turned to face her bureau mirror.

"Oh, geez," she moaned, tugging at the ugly frock. "Look what you've done to me, Miltie! You know that black washes me out something fierce."

She stared at her tired reflection and frowned, pushing out her lower lip.

This wasn't how she'd figured things would end. Never in a million years. She'd had such high hopes when she'd met Milton. He'd been so different from the other men who'd courted her. Courted? Ha! More like who'd taken her for a pitcher of beer at the bowling alley in Alton or groped her at the drive-in movie, like oversexed teenagers.

Her dates with Milton hadn't been like that at all.

He'd treated her like a queen in the beginning. Shots had thought it was because he was so much older, and she'd been kind of tickled, getting involved in one of those May-December affairs. He'd sent her flowers. Okay, so they weren't roses, but they were real nice carnations. He'd wined and dined her at the Outback Steakhouse and had even driven her into St. Louis to the Muny Opera to see "The Music Man."

Sure, he was a little rough around the edges, but she'd found his earthiness endearing. When he'd popped the question during breakfast at IHOP — he'd had the waitress stick the ring in the center of a smiley faced pancake — she'd said "yes" without a moment's hesitation. It wasn't long after that Delilah had come calling. Her hair a bottled red and her face powdered and painted like a middle-aged Barbie, she'd had the nerve to remark, "So this is the best he could do the second time around?" Shotsie had stood there with her mouth hanging open. "I hope you've got money of your own, Miss Whatever-Your-Name-Is," she'd gone on to say. "Because once you and Scrooge have tied the knot, you'll never see another dime as long as he lives."

Shotsie hadn't believed her, of course, not then. It wasn't until about six months after their "I do's" that she'd begun to realize Delilah hadn't just been blowing smoke about Miltie being tight.

She glanced around her, at the clunky furniture that crowded their tiny bedroom. Every piece was old as dirt, left to Milton by his father. Shotsie had seen better at garage sales. Her closet was full of clothes mended so often she felt like a walking rag-bag. This past year, she'd felt lucky if Milt had sprung for take-out chili at the diner once a month.

It never happened this way on TV. She knew all about trophy wives, how their husbands showered them with gifts like diamonds and furs, when all the first wife had gotten was stretch marks and dishpan hands.

Shotsie should have had it made, right?

So how come she felt less like a trophy and more like a paperweight?

Not that Miltie had ever been *bad* to her. He hadn't beaten her or anything. Despite the fact that they'd ended up fighting like cats and dogs, he'd treated her okay. He'd given her stability at least, something she'd never had in all her years growing up.

None of that mattered any more though, did it, now that he was gone?

Tears flooded her eyes, and she brushed them away. She'd end up looking like a raccoon if she didn't stop bawling.

Through the opened window came the gentle chimes of the chapel's carillon, the bells playing "Onward, Christian Soldiers."

Shotsie checked the clock. It was nearly ten o'clock.

Time to get a move on.

She grabbed her purse and made sure it was stuffed with fresh tissues. Then she scurried out of the house she'd shared with Milt for five years. Stumbling over the gravel in her too-tight pumps, she headed for the quaint chapel, its steeple poking the morning sky just a couple blocks away. She quickened her pace, knowing it would hardly look good for the widow to be late.

The closer she got to the church, the more grim-faced townsfolk she bumped into.

"God bless, my dear."

"Be strong, child."

"Keep a stiff upper lip."

"Chin up, young lady, Milton would have wanted it that way."

Oh, yeah? Shotsie thought as she stared into one wrinkled face after another. What Miltie would have wanted was for her to give each one of them a swift kick in the pants.

She entered the vestibule and was instantly greeted by the minister, his square shoulders buried in the folds of a white robe.

"Ah, Mrs. Grone," he said and began describing the order of the service.

He took her hands and led her toward the foremost pew. The nearer they got to the plain pine casket up front, the quieter Fister's voice grew until Shotsie could hardly hear him. She wondered if he was afraid that Miltie might somehow hear and disapprove.

She nearly told him to speak up, that he shouldn't worry. Milton had never cared a fig about religion, not enough to eavesdrop.

The minister left her in front, staring at the casket, and Shotsie started as a hand grasped her shoulder. She swiveled her head to find Helen Evans' kindly face gazing into her own.

"Hello," Helen said and nothing more, something for which Shotsie was grateful. Less was plenty on a day like this, a few honest words better than a string of false condolences.

Shotsie looked past Helen at the rows behind her, every pew completely full.

Clara Foley, Doc and Fanny Melville, the sheriff and his buck-toothed wife, those whack-a-doodle bird-lovers Ida Bell and Dorothy Feeny, even that snotty Felicity Timmons from next door: all had shown up to pay their last respects to Miltie. What a bunch of two-faced phonies! Shotsie ground her lips together, thinking it was enough to make her sick.

The organ music started up, and Shotsie faced forward. She looked over at the ancient instrument and the girl who manned it, Maddy Fister. Sounded like the minister's daughter could use a lesson or two, Shotsie thought with a frown, sniffing as she listened to the halting touch of fingers on keys, feet pumping the pedals below.

Earnest Fister took his place at the carved wooden pulpit, an imposing figure with his brooding features and dark eyes, his arms draped in yards of white. He raised his hands, and the music stopped.

The entire chapel grew still.

"Good morning," he said in his throaty voice, the tiny microphone amplifying his every word. "We've come together today, not to grieve, but to celebrate a very natural part of life . . ."

"Celebrate is right," someone yelled from the back.

Shotsie stiffened and tightened her fingers around the handles of her purse. Oh, no, she thought, it can't be . . .

She heard the clunk of the double doors closing and turned her head slowly to see someone standing in the shadows.

A woman stepped out of the dim alcove and into the well-lit aisle. There, she stopped. Hands on hips, she stuck out her chest and shook her mane of bottle-bought red. From within a face powdered matte white, red lips grinned.

"What are you all staring at?" she said. "Can't a girl attend her own husband's funeral without getting the stink-eye?"

CHAPTER TEN

"Out!" Shotsie's screams filled the church. "Get her out of here!"

Helen gripped the back of the pew, too stunned to move. Silence befell the church for an instant, before voices began buzzing like a hive full of hornets.

"Please, make her go," Shotsie tried again. When her cry went unheeded, she rose from her seat and approached the aisle alone. Fists clenched at her sides, she strode past Helen and then past each row after until she stood nose to nose with the intruder.

"Well, don't you look the part of the grieving widow," Delilah drawled, barely getting all the words out before Shotsie grabbed a hank of red hair.

"Ow! Cut it out!" Delilah shrieked, the grip on her head forcing her to bend. "Hey, somebody, help!"

"For heaven's sake, this is a church, not a playground," the minister intoned, but the women ignored him. Springing out of the pulpit, his robes billowing behind him, he raced toward Shotsie and took hold of her shoulders. "Enough!" he finally shouted.

With a sigh, Shotsie let go.

Delilah groaned as she stood upright and touched her hair with red-tipped fingers. "Thank you, preacher."

Earnest Fister nodded.

"I hate to think this is how all your visitors get treated," she remarked, coaxing her ruined 'do back in place.

"I'm truly sorry, ma'am."

"It's Mrs. Grone," the woman replied and glared at Shotsie. "But you can call me Delilah."

"Grone?" The preacher blinked, glancing from one Mrs. Grone to the other. "But I thought . . ."

"She's the old model," Shotsie said with a smirk. "Milt traded her in years ago. Now make her leave, would you? She wasn't supposed to come in the first place."

Helen had never seen Earnest Fister so flustered, but he was exactly that now. He rubbed his beard, clearly trying to sort things out, before he sighed and told Delilah, "Normally, I'd welcome you into our little chapel with open arms. But, in this case, I must abide by the wishes of the current Mrs. Grone."

Delilah's powdered face crumpled. "Can't I even stand here in the back? It's not like I'm sorry about the old buzzard, but I wouldn't mind sitting in on his send-off. Just to make sure he doesn't rise out of his coffin and flip us the bird."

Fister turned to Shotsie. "Mrs. Grone?"

She shook her head.

The minister faced Delilah again. "Again, I'm sorry, but you'll have to leave."

Frowning, Delilah tugged at her tight sweater and tapped a high-heeled boot. "All right, all right, I'm gone already."

And with a final glance at the closed casket, she slipped through the vestibule's double doors, exiting far more quietly than she'd arrived.

"Mrs. Grone, are you okay?" Reverend Fister led Shotsie back to the front pew. "Then we'll resume."

She nodded, and he returned to the pulpit, hands raised to quiet the murmuring congregation. "As I was saying" — he picked up where he'd left off. "Death is but the completion of the human cycle. It's letting go of our mortal shell and freeing our soul." His gaze traveled over his audience. "It's with this thought in our hearts that we say goodbye to Milton Grone."

Shotsie burst into tears, sobbing so noisily that Fister was forced to pause.

Helen slipped out of her pew and slid into the seat beside Shotsie. Reaching into her purse, she withdrew a neatly folded handkerchief, as Shotsie had managed to dump a mess of tissues from her handbag to the floor. Helen blotted at the trail of tears dripping down the woman's cheeks before pressing the damp kerchief into Shotsie's nail-bitten fingers.

Shotsie seemed calmed by the attention, and sobs turned into hiccups. She quieted enough anyway that Fister was able to continue.

He cleared his throat and shuffled his notes. "What might one say about Milton Grone?" he asked rhetorically though the question merely stirred up another round of whispers. "Was he a giving man? Was he filled with compassion? Was he well-loved?"

A smattering of coughs erupted, and Helen was afraid someone might shout out, "Hardly!" But no one did, and the coughing finally stopped.

"No, my friends," Earnest Fister said, shaking his head and clutching at the edge of the pulpit. "Milton Grone was none of those things. Yet above all, above everything he might have appeared to be, he was a human being with faults and foibles just like the rest of us. He was one of God's children, as deserving of our Good Lord's saving grace as you and me."

Helen kept an eye on Shotsie, who stared hard at the pastor, clearly affected by his words.

". . . no matter who we have been in this life, we are given another chance as we ascend . . ."

Helen found herself focusing on the minister as well, taking in the bearded face, cheeks pink with passion, his eyes as fiery as she'd ever seen them. Beyond him hung an enormous wooden cross, the shape seeming to mimic his own form as he lifted his arms, his robe falling gracefully from each limb; his head and neck as straight as a shaft.

The whine of the organ cranking up sounded like a mournful cry, as a subdued Madeline Fister set her feet to pumping, her fingers poised above the yellowed keys, waiting for the right moment to start.

The girl hadn't donned her uniform of tight skirt and navel-baring shirt this morning, Helen noticed. Instead, Maddy was dressed demurely in a plain navy shift. Her dark hair wasn't sticking up from her head as though she'd poked a finger in a light socket. It was pulled away from her face with a headband. Without an inch of make-up, she appeared younger than her seventeen years and less world-weary. Fragile.

Helen knew the girl had been through a lot in her young life, losing her mother and being raised by a single father, a minister to boot.

Helen wondered how Earnest had managed to keep Maddy under control, what with her penchant for dressing like a hooker. But then, Helen had seen enough TV to know that girls these days sorely lacked for decent role models. It was no wonder, she decided, that so many of them believed being sexy made them more viable.

"Amen," Fister said, his voice a deep rumble.

Helen had missed half the eulogy, and she wasn't sorry.

The pastor signaled to Madeline who pumped her feet faster, her fingers tiptoeing their way through "Nearer my God to Thee."

It was the same tune the band had played when the *Titanic* was sinking, Helen mused with some irony, as she picked up her hymnal and sang along with the rest.

When the hymn had reached its final chorus, Fister came down from the pulpit and approached Shotsie, taking her hands.

"Bless you, my dear," he said solemnly. "Someday you'll see that what's happened was for the best. Let God take care of him now."

“I hope God knows he likes his dinner on the table at six,” Shotsie murmured, her eyes fixed on the coffin. She tugged her hands from Earnest Fister’s grasp and tucked her purse-strap over her shoulder.

Helen thought she looked like she wanted desperately to escape.

But Shotsie would have to wait a while longer to do so, as she was soon surrounded by a swarm of townsfolk, whispering words meant to comfort and patting her back.

Helen eased away from the huddle, making her way through the pews to the aisle on the chapel’s far side.

It was then she noticed that Madeline Fister had risen from the organ bench to take a hesitant step across the dais toward the casket. One foot moved forward and then the other, as if in slow-motion. Her hands brushed at her wrinkled dress then laced together at her belly.

“Be brave, Shotsie . . . if you need anything, please call . . . it will get easier, I promise . . . time heals all wounds, you know . . .”

Helen listened to the sing-song voices and turned briefly toward the thinning crowd around the Widow Grone. Until she heard a loud thump and thought for a moment the heavy cross had come un-nailed from the wall and fallen.

Instead, she saw Madeline Fister crumpled on the floor beside Milton Grone’s coffin, apparently out cold.

CHAPTER ELEVEN

"You'll be as good as new in no time," Doc Melville said, patting Madeline's hand, and she looked up into the smiling faced that hovered above her. His fingers gently touched her wrist, his eyes on his watch as he checked her pulse. Then he patted her again. "Things seem back to normal already."

Normal?

Madeline pressed her eyes closed, afraid the tears that had been building up inside her would suddenly gush freely. Even worse, a wave of nausea engulfed her though she fought it, trying hard to stay calm. She couldn't give in, couldn't break down, not yet. Not in her father's office.

"No doubt it was the strain of the service," Fanny Melville said as she began stroking Madeline's hair, her touch so tentative, as if Maddy were a fragile china doll that might crack. "It's too bad that Emma MacGregor's arthritis was so bad this morning, or else she would have been at the organ and you, sweet girl, could have stayed home."

Maddy's chest tightened suddenly so that she found it hard to breathe. Her heart felt so heavy, like her father's enormous Bible had fallen on top of her, crushing her lungs and ribs.

Oh, God, she thought, it had all been her fault, hadn't it? Would things have been different if she'd kept her secret to herself?

"Are you all right, sweetheart?" Her father's voice no longer seemed so strong and even as it had been throughout the eulogy. There was a catch to it, a trace of fear. Or was it guilt she heard?

She forced her eyes wide open to find him peering down at her anxiously, his skin pale above the gray of his beard. "Can I get you anything?" he asked. "A glass of water?"

"No, I'm fine," she told him and struggled to sit up. She laced her fingers in her lap, pressing her hands together to steady them. "I'm sorry if I caused a scene," she whispered.

"You think *you* caused a scene?" Fanny Melville chuckled. "My dear, you'd have to stand in line for that honor. The two Mrs. Grones are well ahead of you there."

"Maybe it's the flu," another voice suggested, and Maddy caught sight of Helen Evans peeking at her from over Fanny's shoulder. "I've heard there's a vicious strain going around."

Doc scratched his jaw. "She doesn't have a fever, and her pulse is fairly steady. Her throat isn't red, her glands aren't swollen, and her lungs sound clear."

Madeline flushed beneath the scrutiny. She hated how they talked over her as if she wasn't even in the room. All she wanted was to get out of there. To be alone.

"For the tenth time," she told them, "I'm okay. I just got a little dizzy. It's no big deal."

"I'd like you to come in for a full physical," Doc Melville said. "It would hurt to give you a thorough examination."

"No," Maddy said, reacting quickly. She swung her legs off the couch, her knees wobbling as she put her feet on the floor. "It's not necessary, I swear," she added, avoiding her father's eyes. "I'm just tired. I didn't have any breakfast." She'd been too sick to her stomach to eat.

"She'll come in, Doc," her father interjected, and his frightened expression of moments before was gone, replaced by features as firm as granite. "I'll see to it that she gets an appointment."

Madeline wanted to scream at him, to argue that it was *her* life to live, not his. And hadn't he done enough already? But her strength seemed to have left her for now. She stood, brushing away the hands that petted and stroked her, wishing she could run away until this morning was left far behind.

"Can I go?" she said, not caring if she sounded brusque and ungrateful. "Or do you all want to stand around and stare at me all morning?"

"Madeline!"

Her father took hold of her arm, but she pulled free and rushed toward the door. Just as she grabbed the knob, she heard Helen Evans say, "No, Earnest, don't," and then Maddy pushed free and stumbled off.

Tears flooded her eyes so that she could hardly see where she went. She bumped into something and nearly screamed when she realized it was the coffin.

His coffin.

She tripped on the red carpet that ran down the aisle, falling to her knees. She scraped her knees, drawing blood, but she didn't stop.

She scrambled to her feet and forced her legs to move ahead, to get her outside where she could finally breathe; where she didn't have to think of Milton Grone and the last time she'd seen him, wondering if it was her fault that he was dead.

CHAPTER TWELVE

"Well, there you are, Mrs. Evans. I've been waiting for you to come out."

Helen had parted ways with Amos and Fanny Melville a moment before when a curvy figure in high heels popped out from behind a gnarled oak, intercepting her on the sidewalk in front of the church.

"You do remember me, don't you?" the redhead asked, squinting in the sunlight.

"Of course, I do," Helen said. "Hello, Mrs. Grone."

She smiled politely and tucked her purse into the crook of her elbow, thinking the first Mrs. Grone had been a brunette all those years ago. Helen wasn't sure if the red hair was actually flattering, though it did distract a bit from the hard lines around Delilah's mouth and eyes. She had a pinched look on her face as though life had not been kind.

"I haven't seen you around in ages," Helen went on, "not until you showed up at this morning's service. How're you doing? Are you still living in Alton with the boys?"

Delilah pulled a plastic compact from her purse and powdered her nose. "I've got a good job at a restaurant off the highway," she said, "in hospitality."

Hospitality? Helen heard that she waitressed at a truck stop off the interstate.

"My boys are teenagers now, can you believe? It's hard to work full-time and keep 'em in line." Delilah put away her compact and laughed, but there was little amusement in the sound. "You know how kids are these days. They don't listen to a thing their parents say, and it's not like I've had help raising them." She paused and stabbed a hand into her bag, withdrawing a pack of cigarettes. She tapped the bottom and cursed. "Empty," she said, glancing at Helen. "Damn." She crushed the pack in her fist and pocketed the litter. "I guess it's not my day."

Helen felt suddenly sorry for the woman. "Back in the chapel," she began, "if I could apologize for how Shotsie . . ."

"Oh, no, don't bother," Delilah cut her off. "I'm not surprised that Milt's floozy would want me to get the hell out. It's my fault for making an entrance. I should have slipped in and sat down without a peep. I don't know why I do half the things I do sometimes. Milt was always telling me to keep my big trap shut." Delilah tapped a foot on the sidewalk. "The only reason I dropped in was to see for myself if the old coot was dead. I didn't think about how the Black Widow would react." Her painted mouth settled into a grim line. "Not that I imagined she'd be thrilled to see me, but I never thought she'd have me tossed out."

"Shotsie's very upset about losing her husband," Helen said in her defense. "You can't honestly blame her for not wanting you there."

Delilah's hands went to her hips, and her voice prickled with defiance. "Tell me why I shouldn't have come, huh?" The heavily made-up eyes glared at Helen. The crow's feet were hardly disguised by her thick pancake make-up. "No matter how bad things were when Milt and I split, we were married for ten years. We did have two kids together." Her shoulders slumped and, for a moment, she looked away. "It was important for me to be here, you understand. Sort of like watching the last five minutes of a movie to see how it ends."

"Point taken," Helen said, sizing up the former Mrs. Grone and thinking that, despite the physical differences, perhaps she and Shotsie weren't so unalike after all. Both had formed attachments to a man best described as bull-headed. Both seemed deeply affected by his death, despite Delilah's tough facade.

"It's strange to think he won't be around to fight with any more," Delilah said, glancing over at the chapel.

Helen followed the direction of her gaze and saw a pair of men in dark suits emerge from the vestibule. They guided the wheeled contraption upon which Milton's casket lay. They lowered it carefully down the steps and to the curb where a long black hearse awaited. Hardly breaking a sweat, they pushed the casket into the back, the trolley collapsing, and they closed the doors behind it.

Helen read the words printed on the hearse's tailgate: *Morgan & Family. Only the Best for your Beloved's Final Rest.* She shook her head, thinking that advertising showed up in the most inappropriate of places.

"So, his ticker just went out on him all of a sudden, huh?" Delilah said, nibbling on the tip of a red-painted nail. "Then he smacked his head on a rock when he fell." She shuddered. "All that blood. Christ, but it must have been tough for Shotsie to see him lying on the ground like that."

"It was," Helen admitted, finding it difficult to believe that Milton had died just two nights before. "We'd just come from the town meeting and no one was very happy about . . ."

She stopped herself, Delilah's words suddenly striking a chord.

Helen cocked her head. "How did you know he'd struck a rock?"

That tidbit hadn't appeared in the paper, though it was hardly a secret, considering the two dozen townsfolk who'd been present when Milton was found. Still, Helen found it hard to imagine anyone in River Bend phoning Delilah Grone to gossip.

"Well, Mrs. Evans, it's like this," Delilah began, her hands fiddling with the strap of her handbag. "I came to town to meet with Milt that night, of all the rotten timing. I'd been after him for a while to pony up what he owed me. It was only fair, right? I mean, he skipped more child support payments than I could count and forget the alimony!" She let out a noisy *humph*. "I wanted to work something out with him, but Milt wouldn't budge. 'Go on and sue me,' is what he said, and he laughed, like I wouldn't go through with it." Delilah kicked gravel with her shoe, not meeting Helen's eyes. "I called him a dozen times to try to get together but, lately, whenever I phoned, he hung up."

She shifted on her feet and tossed back her red hair, as though trying to shake off bad memories. "It was hard, scraping by, especially when the boys were young. I barely saw a red cent from Milt, and me just working part-time back then. Those were tough days. Real tough."

Helen could only imagine what it had been like. Being a mother had been hard enough with a husband who'd supported her in more ways than one. "Didn't the courts pressure Milton to pay his child support?"

"The courts?" Delilah snorted. "They just shoved me from one social services boob to another. I mean, they apologized right and left, but nobody did a damned thing."

"Certainly Mr. Grone could afford it," Helen said.

"I'll say he could," Delilah replied, and her eyes flashed with anger. "He hardly spent a penny of what he earned, and he'd been working since he was a kid, doing construction and laying down roads for the government. His father didn't help him out so Milton knew how to save his checks. He probably had a bundle earning interest in the bank all these years, and I'm sure he didn't spend it all on Blondie." Her red lips twitched into the hint of a smile. "The old rattrap they live in looks even worse than it did when I left."

Milton's reputation for being miserly was hardly a secret, Helen mused, recalling all the times Art Beaner and the board complained about Mr. Grone refusing to contribute to the community funds that maintained Serenity Gardens, the playground, and the historic lighthouse near the river.

Delilah slapped a hand against her thigh, the noise tugging Helen from her thoughts. "Burns me up, it does," she said, "how Milt could ignore his own flesh and blood like that then go out and strike a big deal for that water park. And don't think I haven't kept up with it in the papers." She tucked her arms beneath her breasts. "That set a fire under me, it surely did, which is why I high-tailed it here after work last Thursday night. I had a few things I wanted to get off my chest even if I had to force the old coot to listen to every word."

Delilah appeared so distraught that Helen pitied her and all she'd had to endure.

"You'd decided to give him an ultimatum, is that it?"

Milton's ex-wife nodded, biting down on her bottom lip.

"He didn't know you were coming?"

"Well, I'd *tried* to warn him," she said. "I called and said, 'okay, Milt, I'm giving you one last chance to make things right,' but he just chuckled. 'And if you don't, I've got someone who'll help me get what I'm after,' I told him. Then he laughed some more before he hung up." She sighed, her voice softening. "I got in my car just after seven o'clock, as soon as I finished my shift. I stopped at home to change clothes so it was probably close to eight when I got to River Bend."

She hesitated, wetting her lips. She cast her gaze down but Helen could plainly see her distress. "I got out of my Bug, and there he was, lyin' on the ground. I walked over and saw for sure that it was Milton. I tried to shake him, telling him to get up. I even knelt down in those damned weeds and got stains on my pants. When I touched his head, I felt something wet, like blood on my fingers. Oh, man, it was awful." She shivered, and Helen reached out to lay a hand on her arm.

"You left without calling for help?"

"I banged on the door to the house, hollering for Shotsie, but no one answered. Then I heard all those voices coming up the street."

"That must have been after the meeting broke up," Helen said. "Ida Bell led a group of, um, concerned citizens to confront Milton about the water park sale."

Delilah swallowed hard. "All I know is that I got out of there fast. I didn't think it would look good for someone to find me hanging around with Milt on the ground as good as dead. They might've thought I had something to do with it."

"Oh, I doubt that," Helen told her with a smile meant to reassure. "He presumably died of a heart attack, as you must know. That could hardly have been your fault."

"Blondie would have found a way to pin it on me, I'm sure. If nothing else, she would have blamed me for causing the bastard's ticker to stop."

Helen didn't respond. Delilah was probably right about that.

The rumble of a car engine coming to life momentarily charged the air, and Delilah stared at something over her shoulder. Helen turned around to see the van from the mortuary driving off in a cloud of exhaust.

"Is she having him cremated?" Delilah asked, her eyes watching the road. "Milt always said he didn't want to be buried, all those worms and stuff."

"I really don't know," Helen told her, her brow creasing as she tried to think of the latest buzz she'd heard this morning. "There won't be any kind of graveside service, I do know that. Doc Melville asked the mortuary to postpone anything until tomorrow."

"Postpone? But why?" Delilah's eyes narrowed. "Is something wrong?"

"No. At least I don't think so." Helen was suddenly anxious to be on her way. "Amos Melville has always been extremely thorough. Could be he's getting a second opinion before it's too late."

"A second opinion?" Delilah repeated, screwing up her face. "Wasn't it a heart attack plain and simple?"

Was anything involving Milton Grone plain and simple? Helen wondered.

She sighed, feeling tired, impatient to get home. Amber was probably using her wicker rocker as a scratching post, furious that she wasn't there to open up a can of tuna. "I'm sorry that I don't have any more answers for you. I'm sure we'll all know soon enough if anything odd turns up though I see no reason why it should."

"You're right, of course," Delilah replied, the pleats in her brow easing somewhat. "Well, it was nice chatting with you, Mrs. Evans." She stuck out her hand, which Helen grasped. "Maybe I'll be back more often now that the old buzzard's gone."

She waved as she teetered along in her high heels, hurrying off in a swing of hips and wiggle of her behind. She headed straight for a beat-up green Volkswagen Beetle, the sort that Helen hadn't seen in years. Hadn't they been banned once a long time ago, she tried to recall, because of the motor being in the back rather than the front? Or was it the Pinto she was thinking of with its gas tank in the rear?

The VW's engine popped and groaned before it finally caught. She looked on as Delilah drove away, wheels grinding over the gravel. And then the Bug went round the corner, out of sight, the motor no more than a fading rattle.

"What an odd bird," Helen thought to herself, shaking her head. My, but Milton Grone certainly had married two real doozies. He'd been a good-looking man if one liked the roughhewn type, but his character had certainly been lacking.

Maybe, she mused as she resumed her walk from the chapel toward her own house, maybe there was a lot more to Milton Grone than anyone had realized.

Though she couldn't imagine what that might be.

As she strolled up the swept sidewalk, she smiled to herself, deciding that if there was any part of Milton's life no one had known, it surely wouldn't take long before someone in River Bend found out.

In a town of this size, secrets didn't stay buried for long.

CHAPTER THIRTEEN

Ida Bell and Dorothy Feeny decamped from Ida's mud-splattered jeep parked on the shoulder of the Great River Road.

There was no footpath carved out before them, not even a dirt road that led onto the property situated barely a half mile up the road from River Bend. The only indication that others had been there recently was a succession of crisscrossing tire tracks, which made parallel lines of mud where weeds and grass had once grown. That, and an enormous billboard perched incongruously before the fog of trees and brush.

FUTURE SITE OF WET 'N' WOOLLY WATER PARK! the sign proclaimed in brilliant blue letters. *Opening next summer!* was added beneath in hot pink.

Merely reading the words made Ida feel sick.

She buoyed her spirits with the thought that Milton Grone was out of the way so there was a chance, however small, that she might put a stop to the construction before it ever came to pass.

Just a few hours after the funeral service, she'd gotten wind of a ceremonial ground-breaking involving several token suits from Wet 'n' Woolly's corporate office, as well as a photographer and reporter dispatched from the *Alton Telegraph*. Rumor had it that a bulldozer hired by the company planned to knock down a small tree or two in a show of force, a promise of how they intended to turn this pristine land into a concrete and plastic jungle despite the small but vocal opposition.

Ida had tried to round up as many of her fellow environmentalists as possible, so that they'd be able to present a strong front against the heartless bullies. She'd spent a better part of the morning, in fact, dialing up one after another of her comrades.

But her watch showed a quarter to twelve already, and, so far, she and Dot were the only ones who'd appeared.

"To think someone could sell all of this for mere money," she said and waved a calloused hand at the copse of trees below the craggy bluffs. She screwed up her face, fighting the sudden urge to spit. "It makes me mad as hell, Dotty. Mad as hell."

"Me, too," Dot chirruped from beside her as they pulled up the jeep's soft cover and retrieved several signs of protest.

Handmade on poster board and stapled onto two-by-fours, Ida's said bluntly: "Murderers!" Though slightly tamer by comparison, Dot's was no less spirited. "Wet 'n' Woolly," she'd written, "Nature's Bully!"

Several additional signs lay in the back of the car, brought along for any of their cohorts who arrived unprepared. Only, it appeared those would go unused.

Ida glanced at her battered watch.

Eight minutes till noon.

She joined Dot in leaning against the hood of the jeep, watching as a dusty pickup or car swept past them in a whoosh of dust and wind, headed up the highway toward Grafton.

"I'll be honest with you, Dot," Ida said, wrinkling her nose as grit from the air settled down on them. "I had a hard time keeping my emotions in check this morning." The white feather-like seeds from cottonwoods blew into her face and stuck in her hair. She didn't bother to brush them out. "It was all I could do not to stand up and cheer during that eulogy of Fister's."

"Ida, watch what you say!" Dot warned her, wide eyes blinking as she glanced around them and then heavenward. "It's bad luck to speak ill of the dead."

Ida snorted. "And why shouldn't I?" she asked. "I never spoke well of him when he was alive. I'd be a hypocrite to do it now."

"Goodness, but that's awfully strong talk," Dot responded and fanned at her flushed cheeks with a liver-spotted hand. "Though it's true, I guess, that no one much liked the man except his second wife."

"Two of a kind, I'd say," Ida remarked. A cottony tuft stuck to her eyelash, and she promptly plucked it off. "She's rotten, too, and no more concerned about the wildlife than he was. I can't help but think it would've saved us a great deal of trouble if she'd joined him on his trip to Hades . . ."

"Ida!" Dot stopped her from going further. "Don't judge the poor woman too harshly," her friend said gently. "It's not her fault the contract's already been signed. The deal has been struck, and there's no going back."

Ida scowled. "That might be true as far as the law's concerned, but it certainly won't stop me from trying to put a halt to this destruction. I'll do whatever I have to, no matter how much blood I get on my hands."

"Ida!" Dot blanched.

"Figuratively, of course," she said.

"I would hope so."

Though Ida knew she'd do whatever it took to stop the construction of Wet 'n' Woolly. She'd grown up around here, had been raised on a farm in Jerseyville, only to move to River Bend when she'd graduated from Illinois Agricultural.

She'd watched as so-called civilization had encroached on the area. Pollution poisoned the air, pumped out of smokestacks from electrical and industrial plants on either side of the river. She ground her teeth, thinking of the waste dumped into the Mississippi waters, lending new meaning to its label as "muddy." It was surely brown as chocolate milk, but hardly safe to drink.

"Don't eat the catfish either," she murmured, remembering when it wasn't toxic to do so. Well, she wouldn't let them ruin this valley so near to her home. She wouldn't let them destroy the habitat of countless owl, deer, and rabbit.

"After all," she declared, "the animals can't speak for themselves. So someone must, and that someone is me."

"I'm with you, don't forget." Dot poked a finger in the air.

Ida glanced at her sideways. "No, I doubt if I could ever make that oversight."

The noisy growl of an engine came into her earshot, and Ida edged around the Jeep, squinting at the van that approached.

"Ah-ha." It was the boys from the *Telegraph*. She held her sign up and nudged Dot, who raised hers high as well.

The van pulled off the road and onto the shoulder ahead of the Jeep. Its doors came open and two men emerged. A big black camera hung from the neck of one, a tall sort in blue jeans and ponytail; the other, fat and freckled, flipped open a notepad.

"Hey, look who it is, Tom," the reporter said to his buddy. "Nice to see you again, Miss Bell. It is Bell, isn't it?" he asked, scribbling across the paper. He glanced up at her, grinning like the Cheshire cat. "B-e-l-l," he spelled out, "as in ding-dong?"

Ida stiffened.

The men laughed.

"Please, don't attack him like the last time," Dot whispered, and Ida tightened her grip on the two-by-four.

A thunderous noise rent the air, drowning out Ida's dark thoughts. She turned toward the sound as did the others. She quickly spotted a dirt-splattered bulldozer moving up the highway toward them. A fellow in orange hardhat sat at its helm, working the gears.

The ground shook beneath Ida's feet as the tractor came nearer, finally veering off the road and onto a spot very near Ida's jeep. Behind it, a black Mercedes sedan glided onto the shoulder and parked.

The air vibrated as the bulldozer idled, the cacophony nearly drowning out the voices of the men who got out of the car from the back. Their driver rolled down his window and lit up a cigarette, but otherwise stayed put.

"Let's make it quick," a thin man in a boxy gray suit and red tie loudly barked to the younger chap at his elbow.

"Yes, sir, will do. As fast as we can," his assistant bobbed his head and scurried round to the trunk to withdraw a shovel. Then he led the way for the impatient executive, picking a path through the knee-high weeds toward the billboard.

The reporter and photographer followed.

Sign in hand, Ida went after them, Dot bringing up the rear.

Red Tie snarled when he saw the two women. "What're they doing here?" he shouted at the man with the shovel. "Where'd they come from?"

Ida took a step forward. "We're from God's green earth," she said, before the young fellow could reply. "We're to protect what's rightfully ours."

"Rightfully yours?" The suit stared at Ida. His eyes narrowed in disgust. He turned to his assistant and jerked a thumb. "Who the hell's that?"

"She's a protestor, Mr. Ridgely."

"I can see that, Johnson."

"It's best to ignore them, sir."

Cheeks flushed, Ridgely nodded and reached up to fiddle with the knot of his tie. "Yes, ignore them," he repeated. "How much damage could two little old ladies cause." He snapped his fingers at the pair from the *Telegraph*, and they hurried to his side like anxious pups.

Ida lowered her sign and stood in silence, fuming as she watched the Wet 'n' Woolly executive pose for a picture, beaming like he'd won the Mega-Millions lottery. The large blue and pink sign provided a vivid backdrop behind him as he pressed the tip of the shovel to the dirt. He propped the toe of a leather oxford gingerly atop the metal spade, as if about to push the blade into the ground.

Several yards away, the bulldozer waited for the go-ahead, the groan of its motor like a growling pit-bull straining at its leash.

The reporter jotted down whatever Ridgely's assistant was telling him, while the photographer moved from one spot to the next, getting shots from all possible angles.

At Ida's elbow, Dot sighed noisily. "I guess he's right," she said. "What could a couple of antiques like us do to a big corporation like Wet 'n' Woolly? We might as well go on home now. It is time for lunch."

Ida didn't answer.

She held her head high and the sign even higher. She fixed her gaze dead-ahead on one man in particular, unwilling to bend.

"Ida, I said maybe we should go back . . ."

"Did MacArthur throw in the towel," she argued under her breath. "Did Eisenhower capitulate? Did Lee?" she uttered, every muscle within her thin body tensed.

"But Lee surrendered at Appomattox," Dot told her and poked her side.

Ida swatted at her. "Pish posh!" she hissed and shook with indignation. "I will not be defeated, not now nor ever, do you hear me? I won't let them win. I won't!"

"Ida, be reasonable . . ."

But reasonable was the farthest thing from Ida's mind.

Tossing aside her handmade sign, she strode forward, her riding boots crashing through the high grass.

"Ida, wait!"

But she did not slow her steps or back away when the red-tied Ridgely scowled and screamed at her: "Take your friend and get off this land, old woman, or I'll have you arrested for trespassing!"

Ida forged ahead, undeterred, brushing off the pale hand of Johnson as he stammered for her to, "Please go, ma'am, please."

Still Ida didn't hesitate. She stopped only when she stood before Ridgely, staring fearlessly into his face, red with fury.

Then she lunged forward, grabbing the wooden handle of the shovel so that he was jerked off-balance. His foot, once propped atop the metal spade, came up from beneath him.

"Now maybe you'll listen!" Ida told him, the rise of her voice causing a nest of blue jays to squawk from the branches of a tree above. She brought the shovel up over her shoulder and swung it down like a hatchet.

Dot screamed.

Ridgely flung his arms over his head.

A hand reached out from behind her and grabbed her arm, deflecting the shovel from its mark.

But not before the *Telegraph's* photographer snapped a shot of Ida attacking Wet 'n' Woolly's senior vice-president.

"I could sue you for assault and battery, you crazy hen!" Ridgely shouted as Ida marched undaunted toward the Jeep. A string of curses reached her ears as she tossed the signs into the back of the car, not bothering to fasten the soft cover.

"Come along, Dot," she said to her wide-eyed cohort, climbing up and into her seat behind the wheel.

With a squeal of tires, she pulled the Jeep onto the highway, U-turning across the yellow line between the lanes. Then she headed away from the construction site, racing back to town; thinking all the while that it was too bad she'd been stopped from banging that foul-mouthed Ridgely on top of his fat head.

It might have rid the world of one more despicable fellow.

CHAPTER FOURTEEN

Sunday dawned with nary a storm cloud on the horizon. The air seemed oddly calm, Helen thought, peaceful after the rather turbulent days that had preceded it.

The bells from the chapel clanged promptly at eight and then again at half-past when the morning service was to start.

The half-dozen members of the church choir stood on the dais singing "The Garden of Prayer" as Helen entered in the company of Clara Foley and Lola Mueller.

Fanny and Amos Melville greeted them as they passed through the vestibule. The pair handed out copies of the morning's program and welcomed all with warm hellos.

Madeline Fister sat at the helm of the old organ again, and Helen supposed Emma MacGregor must still be having those arthritis flare-ups. The girl played in the same hesitant manner as she had the day before. Helen wondered if she felt no better than she had at Milton's funeral.

She slipped into a pew midway up the aisle, scooting in beside Clara. Within another few minutes, the place had nearly filled up.

The choir sung the final chorus of the hymn, the bird-like soprano and bullfrog bass of their voices trailing off. There was a moment of relative quiet, of rustling programs and whispers, before Earnest Fister emerged from the door to the right of the dais and approached the pulpit. He was draped in his familiar white robe, his bearded countenance as solemn as ever.

"Good morning," he said.

"Good morning, Dr. Fister," Helen said, joining in with the congregation's dutiful reply.

He shuffled the notes he'd set to the side of a Bible stuffed with bookmarks. "I'd like to thank you all for coming on this particular Sunday. I know the past several days have been hard on all of us so it's especially good to see you here." He nodded, but Helen saw no trace of a smile. "I'd also like to thank my daughter, Madeline," he added, gesturing at the teenager. "She's agreed to play for us again, as Emma's still not up to par, though she's certainly in our prayers."

Helen glanced up from her seat in the sixth row, peering between the heads before her. Madeline Fister did not acknowledge her father's words. Indeed, she sat on the bench at the organ, her hands in her lap, eyes downcast.

She looked, Helen thought, truly miserable. Her complexion was sallower than yesterday if that was possible. Her hair hung limply in her eyes without a headband to restrain it. The dark strands fell about her like a half-drawn curtain.

"I think a most appropriate theme for this morning's sermon is truth," Fister said and paused to clear his throat. Then he gripped the pulpit with both hands. "In these difficult times we live in, it seems that this much-valued quality of truth has become more and more elusive. What we find in its stead is dishonesty. Lies. Empty promises that can never be fulfilled." His voice slipped into its soothing monotone, the sound of it so lulling that Helen was tempted to close her eyes and nod off.

Beside her, Clara Foley yawned unabashedly, stirring up the hair on the head of the fellow in pew before her. Helen gave Clara a nudge, and she covered her open mouth with the palm of her hand.

"Why is it so hard for us to be honest with each other? Why does it seem so impossible to be our true selves every minute of each day instead of donning masks for different occasions?" Fister asked, and his dark eyes swept across the room. "Can we halt the spread of lies," he went on, "and instead speak only what is real, what is right?"

Helen found herself looking down at her hands, and she fiddled with her wedding ring. Clara shifted her rather ample rear end, bumping Helen and muttering an apology before she stopped fidgeting. Helen heard a smattering of coughs and then what sounded like a snore.

"Mark, Chapter Four," Fister said and tapped a finger to the thick Bible before him as he read: "And he said to them, 'Is there a lamp brought to be put under a bushel, or under a bed, and not on a stand? For there is nothing hid, except to be made manifest; nor is anything secret, except to come to light . . .'"

Despite how hard she tried to focus, Helen's mind wandered, and she glanced at those around her. She thought of Milton Grone's widow and wondered if she'd attended the service. Though she sought out the frizzy blond mop that identified Shotsie Grone, she couldn't find her. Helen knew she hadn't seen Grone's widow upon entering the chapel. Perhaps, Shotsie had come in late and slipped into a pew further back. Or, more likely, she hadn't come at all. Milton had never been a churchgoer, and Shotsie had always seemed to follow his lead.

Delilah had not lived quite as much in Milton's shadow. She'd made quite an impression on the town after she'd wed Milt several decades ago. Before their children had been born, she'd tried joining the bridge club for a spell and had once volunteered at the annual bake sale. But her attempt to blend in had been brief and ineffective.

Shotsie had been more invisible. Many townsfolk had not even known what Milton's second wife looked like until a year or more after the couple had married.

Helen tried to recall if Milton Grone had ever attended a town meeting. After a moment's pause, she nodded as a vivid image came suddenly to mind. On a Thursday night after Gerald Grone had died, Milton strode into town hall and interrupted the proceedings. He'd nearly caused a brawl when he'd told he gathered crowd that the land promised to River Bend by his father was not theirs at all but his. They had no document to back up their claim so the property was his inheritance, he'd insisted. And if they wanted it, they'd have to pony up a seven-figure sum.

It was but three days ago that Shotsie had popped into a Thursday night meeting and nearly started a fistfight with Ida Bell.

Helen sighed quietly, finding it disturbing that two generations of Grone men had died, leaving townsfolk feuding over the same patch of land.

Only, this time, there would be no question about to whom that land belonged. Milton had closed the deal with Wet 'n' Woolly weeks ago, though that hardly put a stop to the opposition. And no one, she decided, was more opposed than Ida Bell.

She smiled, remembering the photograph she'd seen on the front page of that morning's *Alton Telegraph*: Ida with a shovel raised high in the air, looking mad as hell. Below her a balding man cringed, arms outstretched.

FOR WHOM THE BELL TOLLS, the caption had read, going on in smaller print to say, "Naturalist Ida Bell Threatens Wet 'n' Woolly Veep during Ground-breaking."

Oh, Ida! She felt a bubble of laughter tickle her throat, though she fought to suppress it. It would hardly do for her to erupt into giggles in the midst of Dr. Fister's sermon.

Settling her hands in her lap, Helen tried to be good.

"Despite what television and the movies seem to be telling us, that children are cute when they lie, that it's amusing to deceive, we must realize deep within ourselves that it simply isn't so. We must teach our children that to hide the truth is wrong, that to prevaricate is harmful. As it says here in Proverbs . . ."

Once again, Helen's mind drifted, and she found herself staring at Madeline Fister seated at the organ.

The girl didn't look at all well, she decided. She seemed to sway upon the stool, and her hands gripped the sides of the organ to hold herself steady. Helen worried that she might collapse again, but she did not fall. Instead, she lifted her head higher as her father gave a nod, and she pumped her feet, plucking out the notes to "Lead, Kindly Light."

Her strokes did not flow so much as hesitate every now and again, so that the voices who sung appeared to pause along with her and then speed up again.

Clara gave her a nudge, and Helen fixed her gaze on the hymnal held open in Clara's plump hands. "Lead, kindly light, amid the encircling gloom," she sang along, wincing as her friend's tremulous falsetto rang painfully in her ear.

". . . the night is dark, and I am far from home . . ."

Maddy stumbled on a wrong note, and Helen's voice flagged with the rest of the congregation until the girl found her way once more.

". . . the distant scene, one step enough for me. Ahh-men."

The congregation drew out the last word, the organ winding down, and Fister resumed his sermon, adroitly turning talk of truth and light into the subject of donations.

Right on cue, a pair of men rose from their seats in the foremost pew, going forward to the dais to collect two gilded plates from the minister. The choir stood as well and formed two neat rows beside the pulpit. While they harmonized to yet another inspirational piece, the pair of men went about the collection.

Madeline hunched over the keys, her face slick beneath the lights. Her fingers stuttered and stammered though she covered up her mistakes well enough for most not to have noticed. After all they were used to Emma MacGregor, who was hardly a virtuoso where the pump organ was concerned. Emma made errors often, though no one was ever unkind enough to remark upon them. Helen found it amazing that a woman whose fingers were constantly swollen with arthritis could still play as well as she did and on so many Sunday mornings.

When the song concluded, Helen saw Madeline rise to her feet and dash through the door that led to Fister's office.

She glanced around her, but no one else seemed startled by the girl's departure. In fact, she doubted if any had noticed as the choir dispersed to their seats and the pair passing the plates still moved about.

Was she truly ill? Helen wondered, her eyes shifting to Fister standing in his robes at the pulpit, his somber face focused on the pages of the opened Bible.

Did the child need help?

Madeline *was* seventeen soon to be eighteen, she reminded herself. Hardly a baby. Should the girl want assistance, she'd no doubt ask for it. Though her decision left her feeling uncomfortable, Helen stayed put until the service ended.

Dr. Fister closed his Bible and stepped off the dais, leading an exodus from the church.

Helen remained inside, moving against the departing crush, and edged her way up the aisle, past the pulpit, and through the door by which Madeline had made her escape fifteen minutes earlier.

"Maddy?" she said, as she looked across the cramped room: at the old wooden desk where Earnest Fister no doubt sat to compose his various lessons, and at the overstuffed couch and end tables topped with mismatched lamps. Then her eyes went to the stained-glass window. The sun penetrated the colored panes, touching the plain pine planks below with a prism-like rainbow.

She stared at the depiction of the Virgin and baby Jesus, and thought suddenly of the day when the window had been put in. There'd been a lengthy renovation of the chapel, something Gerald Grone had done his part to finance. New floorboards had replaced rotting ones, electrical outlets were repaired, sturdy shingles covered a once-leaky roof, and fresh exterior paint lent brightness to a facade which had, over the years, cracked and peeled.

"Donated by Gerald and Eda Grone," the bronzed plaque beneath the window read, and Helen shook her head, wondering what Gerald and Eda would think of Milton's deal with Wet 'n' Woolly. She doubted their reaction would be anything but sad.

A small noise cut into her consciousness, and she turned around, thinking she heard a voice. Had someone called out?

The door to the attached bath stood slightly ajar. Helen could see no light on inside, but again heard the sound. It was rather like a low moan, a stifled cry.

Without further pause, she hurried to the door and pushed it wide.

There on the floor lay Madeline curled into a fetal position. Her dark hair stuck to skin damp with sweat. Her thin arms hugged her knees. Her body convulsed, and a groan escaped her lips, though she pressed her wrist to her mouth and bit down on the joint like a gag.

"Oh, my," Helen murmured. "You poor thing."

The girl moaned again, and Helen set aside her purse and knelt down. She brushed back the stringy hair exposing Maddy's frightened eyes, her delicate features contorted with pain.

"Child, what's wrong?"

Maddy's eyes welled with tears. At Helen's touch on her feverish brow, the tears broke loose. "I . . ." she tried to get out, but another spasm shook her. She squeezed her eyes shut until it passed. "The baby," she uttered between sobs so tremulous Helen wasn't sure she'd heard right.

"The baby," Maddy breathed, "something's wrong."

Helen stiffened.

"Please, help me."

"Hold on, dear, hold on," Helen told her quite firmly, slipping her purse beneath the girl's head. Then she rose to her feet, hurrying toward the door and through the chapel as fast as her legs would carry her.

CHAPTER FIFTEEN

The chapel slowly emptied out. Just a dozen lingered inside, chatting as they waited to pass through the vestibule doors. Earnest Fister stood outside on the steps, bidding his parishioners good-day.

To Helen's relief, she saw Fanny and Amos Melville bringing up the rear of the line. Since they'd greeted at the door this morning, they'd apparently waited until all had gone before retrieving the potted chrysanthemums that decorated the pulpit.

Before Helen had even called to her, Fanny turned and saw her coming. A potted mum in her arms, she elbowed Amos, and they started walking, meeting Helen halfway up the aisle.

"You're white as a ghost," Fanny said, peering over her spectacles. "What's going on?"

"It's Maddy," Helen said, her heart thumping. She held onto a pew and paused, catching her breath. "She's in bad shape."

"What happened?" Amos set down the pot of mums he carried. "Did she have another dizzy spell?"

Helen shook her head. "It's more than that," she told them, as Fanny put down her mums as well. "Please, hurry,

Doc," she urged, leading the pair toward Fister's office. "I think she's having a miscarriage."

"Miscarriage?" Doc stopped in his tracks.

Fanny's eyebrows went up but she said nothing, merely prodded Amos on.

Madeline lay as before on the bathroom floor, holding her knees to her chest, moaning and trembling.

"Let's take a look at you," Doc Melville said and quickly got down on a knee beside her. He fished out a penlight from inside his jacket and peered into Maddy's eyes. Then he put away the light and set his fingers to her wrist.

Helen kneaded her hands together as Doc shook his head.

"Bear with me, Maddy," he said and tugged at the waist of Madeline's skirt, baring her abdomen. Pressing his palm to her belly, his brow furrowed in concentration.

He sighed as he set her waistband to rights and turned to his wife. "We've got to get her to my office," he said, his voice calm but urgent. "She needs real medical attention."

"Can you help her, Amos?" Fanny asked.

"I can help ease her pain, but what's happening is not something I can fix," he said, grunting as he hooked an arm under Madeline's knees and another beneath her spine.

"Why, Amos, you can't carry her," Fanny scolded, but Doc struggled to his feet, huffing and puffing, his face red with strain as he shuffled through the door and past them.

Helen followed him into the chapel with Fanny not far behind. They were halfway up the center aisle, when Earnest Fister came in through the vestibule doors.

He froze when he saw Maddy in Doc's arms. He looked at Helen, but didn't speak, not even to question. Instead, he stepped up to Amos and took the girl from him, cradling her against his chest.

While Doc got the door, Fister hurried out of the church and down the stone steps. He avoided the clusters of people still loitering on the grounds. Instead, he cut around the side yard, taking a footpath through a wooded lot and emerging at the street on its other side.

Helen could hardly keep up with him any more than Amos or Fanny.

The minister had already let himself into Doc's office by the time Helen and the Melvilles arrived.

As Fanny went about flipping on the lights, Amos headed back to the examining room where Fister had settled his daughter upon a cushioned table. Helen peered at them from the doorway, hearing as Fister asked if he could stay.

"I'd rather you didn't," Doc answered and looked up at Helen. At his nod, she touched the pastor's arm and steered him away.

She took him to the waiting area and made him sit. By then, Fister's face had gone ashen. His eyes looked petrified.

Her heart went out to him, and she took his hand, patting it. "She'll be just fine, I'm sure," she told him, summoning up a brave smile for his benefit. "Doc will take good care of her."

Fister pulled away, his white robe rustling about his agitated figure as he paced the room, rubbing his hands together as though trying to warm them. "She looked so broken," he said then and paused with his back to her. "I've never felt so scared," he added in a whisper, drawing his palms to his face. "Never."

Helen went to his side, touching his shoulder. "Amos is the best there is. You've nothing to worry about."

"Don't I?" He turned. His dark eyes bore into hers, his stare so piercing she found it hard not to flinch. "She'll lose the baby, won't she?" he asked bluntly, taking Helen aback.

"She was pregnant?"

Fister nodded.

"You knew?" Helen wondered how it had pained him to keep such a secret.

"Yes," he said, anguish flooding his voice.

"She told you?"

"No," he said, and his broad shoulders slumped. "But I suspected from the way she was acting, and I did know of the affair," he faltered, his head dropping to his chest. "She mentioned seeing someone older. She thought it was serious." His gaze met Helen's. "It wasn't, not for him." Fister's hands curled to fists. "I put an end to it and, God help me, I'm glad I did. I should have called the sheriff but Maddy begged me not to. She said she'd never forgive me if I did. I wish I had, before I made things even worse." He paused, drawing in a deep breath. "I've never felt such hatred before, such anger. I couldn't just stand around and let it go on."

"She's young, Earnest. Give her time. The two of you will work this out . . ."

He shook his head. "She's been growing apart from me for a long time now. I didn't want it to happen. No matter what I did . . . how hard I tried . . ." He threw up his hands, letting out a slow breath. "If her mother had been here, perhaps Maddy wouldn't have sought out someone so wrong for her. I can't help but wonder if she did it to punish me."

"Earnest," Helen said gently to stop him from beating himself up. "This isn't your fault. Maddy's nearly eighteen, and she's not naive. Surely, she realized the consequences of her relationship. There wasn't anything you could have done to stop her if her mind was made up."

"But I'm a minister of God," he said, sliding into a vinyl-covered seat near the wall. "I should have been a better teacher."

Helen sat down beside him. It unnerved her to see the usually stoic man so torn apart. She had thought of him as stronger somehow because of his height and the shoulders that seemed doubly wide beneath his robes. Inside, though, he was as human as the rest of them. Even those standing on pedestals could easily fall. "I'm sorry to say that no one's exempt from the trials of raising a teenager, not even the clergy."

He leaned his brow upon his hands, pressed together as if in prayer. "Perhaps you're right," he whispered.

"Of course, I am. I had four of them."

He rose from the chair and crossed the room to stare out the window. He laced his fingers together and tucked down his chin, standing in silence.

Helen knew how much he must hurt, how this affair of Maddy's had turned his world upside-down.

She sat there quietly, checking her watch now and again, though it was half and hour at least before Doc appeared in the hallway. His white hair askew on his brow, he peeled latex gloves from his hands and approached.

Helen stood.

Fister turned at his footsteps. "Madeline?" he said, dark eyes hopeful. "How is she?"

"She's exhausted. Fanny is with her."

"Can I see her?"

Doc nodded. "Let her rest for an hour then I'll drive you both home."

Fister brushed past Helen and disappeared through the doorway.

"Did she miscarry?" Helen asked.

Doc nodded wearily. "There wasn't much I could do, except try to make it as easy for her as possible."

"How far was she along?"

"Couldn't have been more than about eight weeks."

"Maybe it was for the best," Helen murmured, hating the words even as she said them. She glanced up. "She was so young. She'll have children someday when she's ready."

Doc looked down the hall and then at Helen. "The pastor, how is he?"

"He knew she was pregnant," Helen said. "But I don't think anyone else does."

"It's a private matter," Doc said and frowned. "The girl doesn't deserve to be the fodder of local gossip."

"I won't say a word."

"And neither will Fanny," Amos said. When Helen lifted an eyebrow, he scowled. "She's been a doctor's wife for fifty-odd years. Surely, she's learned to keep a secret by now."

So apparently had Maddy, Helen thought, recalling Fister's words about his daughter's affair, a relationship he'd broken up though, apparently, not soon enough.

And though it was none of her business, Helen couldn't help but wonder who Maddy Fister's secret, older boyfriend was.

CHAPTER SIXTEEN

Felicity Timmons went home from the chapel after Sunday service and traded her silk dress for a floral duster and dirt-stained tennis shoes. She pinned a straw hat to her cropped gray hair, then left the dim of her house for the bright of outdoors.

She'd neglected to clean her gardening tools these past few days. What with Milton's death and then his funeral yesterday, she'd fallen off her regular routine and thought it high time she got right back on.

Round to the patio she went to retrieve the trowels she'd used to plant her marigolds the other afternoon. Taking the tiny shovels by their green handles, she brought them over to the spigot where she rinsed off each, picking at the most stubborn bits of dried earth with her closely-clipped fingernails. That accomplished, she used an old towel to dry them before storing them away until the next time.

Whistling cheerily, she went to fetch the shovel she'd leaned up against the lattice late last Thursday night.

Ah, last Thursday.

The tune faded from her lips. Her feet seemed suddenly stuck to the sod.

It was the last she'd seen Milton Grone alive.

She looked over at the fence he'd built and a shiver ran through her.

For there stood Shotsie in the unkempt yard at the spot where they'd found her husband. She had her hands on her hips, but Felicity couldn't see her face, what with her standing in the shadows of an overgrown oak.

Should I speak up, she wondered? Should I say "hello," out of politeness if nothing else. But her mouth felt so dry she couldn't get a word out. She lifted a hand, but Shotsie turned her back and went inside.

A trickle of sweat slid from her brow to the slope of her nose, and Felicity brushed it away. Where was her spine? Good God, she'd survived being dumped at the altar and moving halfway across the globe, and here she was falling apart at the mere sight of that woman.

She straightened her shoulders.

All right, Felicity told herself, what was done was done, and she wouldn't feel guilty for it.

Putting both Milton and Shotsie out of her mind, she dusted off her hands and sighed. She felt suddenly angry at herself for letting Milton Grone affect her so, even in death, when she should be relishing the fact that he could no longer bother her.

She could enjoy her gardening again; truly revel in the pleasures of getting her hands brown with dirt. She could plant as many bushes near the fence as she saw fit without worrying about them being "accidently" sprayed with herbicide. The roses she'd planted near the road out front could safely bloom without fear of being flattened by Milton's pickup. Even her old tabby, Kitty, could roam about without concern at being the target of Milt and his bloody shotgun.

A childhood tune came to her lips, and she began to hum as she went in pursuit of the shovel. The sun sliced through the boughs of her old oaks, and she reveled in the warmth. Her hum became singing, and "Ring Around the Rosey" perkily emanated from her lips as she headed toward where the shovel had been leaning on the lattice of the porch.

Only, it wasn't there.

She walked back and forth, from one end of the porch to the other, twice.

The song died in her throat, and she turned in a circle, looking all around her.

Where in the blazes could her shovel have gone? It had hardly gotten up and walked away. It had to be around somewhere.

She scrutinized the lattice beneath the porch and then walked around the house itself, looking beneath bushes and behind trellises, but saw no sign of it.

"Bollocks," she said, throwing up her hands, knowing that somehow, some way, her shovel had vanished.

In all the years she'd lived in this town, she'd never had anything stolen, nothing but a few flowers picked by a passerby.

She sunk down on her porch steps, feeling strangely sad, far more distressed at losing the old tool than she was at what happened to Milton.

CHAPTER SEVENTEEN

Amos Melville had just gotten his office back to himself and settled down behind his desk when the telephone rang. He picked it up. "Yes?"

"I didn't sleep a wink last night, my friend, but I got you the answers you wanted. I'm not sure, though, that you'll be so anxious to hear them."

Amos sighed, sure then that he'd made a big mistake.

"Give it to me straight, Ed." Amos eyed the patient files stacked on his desk as he listened to Dr. Drake lay out his findings from Milton Grone's autopsy.

Amos didn't interrupt, not once, merely punctuated the information dealt him with a murmur of, "ah-ha" or "I see."

When Drake had finished, Doc took off his glasses and rubbed the bridge of his nose. "So, you'll get a copy of your report to me as soon as possible?"

"I'll drop it by myself this afternoon, if you'd like."

"Great," Doc mumbled to himself as much as Drake, "I'll have to amend the death certificate. The body's set to be cremated tomorrow."

"I'm sure his friends at least will be glad to know the truth."

Doc let out a dry laugh. "The man didn't have any friends."

And, he mused, those who knew Milton best likely wouldn't care about the truth, just the fact that he was dead and out of their hair forever.

"He was a mean bugger, eh? Well, that makes sense enough," Drake replied. "From the looks of his crushed temporal lobe, your Mr. Grone pissed someone off pretty bad."

"Oh, he pissed off a lot of someones," Doc said.

"Wish I had better news."

"Thanks for your help, Ed," Amos said, parting after a mention of a golf date the next weekend.

When he hung up, Doc couldn't focus on the mountain of files on his desk that needed dictation. He could think only of what Drake had confirmed in these five minutes past.

"It's my professional opinion that Milton Grone's death wasn't caused by his heart but by a blow to his skull . . ."

Something Amos had suspected when he'd examined the body.

"The tissue from his heart showed damage all right, but it wasn't recent. You mentioned a severe myocardial infarction that kept him in the hospital years ago. I'll bet it's related to that. I'd put my money on the skull fracture killing him. I found particles of iron oxides mixed with brain matter so it looks like a hard metal object."

Drake's words ran through his head, and Amos shifted in his chair.

"Chemical analysis also identified dirt, rust, and traces of a nitrogen, calcium, phosphorus, and potassium compound."

What the hell?

"Fertilizer," Drake had told him. "What the green-thumbs stir in with their topsoil to make their plants grow."

Fertilizer?

Amos stared ahead at the wall, so deep in his own thoughts he didn't realize he wasn't alone until he heard a voice.

"Are you okay?" It was Fanny.

He started to lie and tell her, "I'm fine." Then he shook his head. "No. No," he told her. "I'm not okay, not by a long shot."

She crossed her arms and waited for him to go on.

"Got a call from Ed Drake," he said, knowing how Fanny liked things straight-up, no pussy-footing around. "It appears that Milt was killed by a blow to the head. He didn't die of a heart attack, Fanny. He was murdered."

"What?"

He nodded.

Before he'd said another word, his wife had picked up the phone and dialed. "Hello," he heard her say, "Sheriff? I think you'd better get over here stat."

CHAPTER EIGHTEEN

Helen parked her Chevy on the graveled road in front of the gingerbread Victorian, the car knocking back several times as she turned off the ignition.

Felicity had called her earlier in the afternoon, asking if she'd mind taking a trip into Wal-Mart. She needed to replace some of her gardening tools, she'd said. As Helen hadn't been engaged in anything more pressing than the Sunday morning crossword, she had agreed to drive and had immediately grabbed her purse.

They'd stayed in Jerseyville but an hour or so, leisurely rolling a cart up and down Wal-Mart's aisles, which Helen found caused her to end up buying half a dozen things she didn't know she needed until she saw them.

All the ever-practical Felicity had purchased was what she'd gone there to get in the first place: a new shovel. It was nestled in the trunk of the car alongside Helen's three bags full of various gadgets, cleaners, shampoos, and curtain rods.

"Let me carry this for you," she offered as she popped the trunk and removed the heavy spade.

But Felicity merely threw back her thin shoulders and told her, "Nonsense! I'm strong as an ox, which you well know. I've only a year on you besides, so, if you'd hand it over . . ."

"Here you go," Helen said, though she was tempted to utter, "Yes, sir!" and salute. Felicity seemed full of vim and vigor again as though losing her ornery next-door neighbor had given her a second wind.

"Come along," Felicity trilled and slung the shovel over her shoulder. "I'll fix us each a cuppa if you'd like to join me."

"Love to."

From beneath her hat brim, Felicity smiled. Her finely-lined skin crinkled merrily. "After all," she remarked, "we've something to celebrate."

"Celebrate?" Helen pushed down the trunk, leaning on it as she looked up at Felicity. She saw her friend glance across the way toward the Grone house, the grin tightening on her mouth, and then she understood.

"Maybe now I'll have some peace," Felicity said, her voice hushed. "Shotsie's loss is my blessing."

Helen sighed, "Felicity . . ."

"No, Helen, don't look at me so. The man was a bloody ogre, and you know it. If only Gerald had done as he'd promised and left all his land to the town then his son might never have come back. Then he'd never have bothered any of us."

"Wishing doesn't change anything," Helen reminded her.

Her eyes still on the house beyond the fence, Felicity frowned. "To think Milton sold that gorgeous patch of valley and bluff to a water park. Pah," she spat. "They might as well build a shopping mall as well."

Helen couldn't help smiling. "You'd better not say that too loud or Shotsie might hold out for a shopping mall, too."

"Good heavens!" Felicity grabbed the handle of the shovel and ambled up the cobbled path toward her front porch. She left the shovel near the steps, before ascending and holding opening the screened door for Helen.

The crunch of approaching tires on gravel caused Helen to turn. The dusty black-and-white that belonged to Sheriff Biddle rolled up the road toward Felicity's house.

"What's he doing here?" Felicity said, a slight quiver in her voice.

But the car bypassed Felicity's Victorian, coming to a stop in front of the Grone's dented mailbox. Biddle emerged from the driver's side, hiking up his pants. Doc appeared from the passenger side, lending a hand to Fanny who scrambled out of the back.

Felicity sighed; clearly relieved Biddle hadn't come for her.

"Sheriff!" Helen called, waving as she scurried toward the road. "What's going on?" she asked, approaching the trio standing on the edge of the Grone's weed-infested yard.

Amos and Fanny looked at the sheriff then back at each other, seemingly unwilling to spill the beans.

Finally, Biddle hooked his thumbs in his utility belt and stepped forward. "Well, it's like this, ma'am," he said, clearing his throat. "Doc just got a call from his friend at the county medical examiner's office. Dr. Drake ran some additional tests on Mr. Grone."

"And?" Helen prodded. Her eyes went to Amos. "It wasn't a heart attack, was it?"

Amos frowned.

"Looks that way, ma'am," the sheriff said what Amos wouldn't.

"Oh, for Pete's sake," Fanny said with a sniff. "Helen might as well find out now. It'll get around town soon enough. His heart didn't kill him. His head did."

"His head?"

"He didn't strike that rock when he fell like Amos initially thought. Somebody hit him hard with a blunt object. Whoever did it must've moved the body and put Milton there with his skull on the stone."

"How can that be?" Helen asked, as a chill washed over her. "It simply can't be true. No one in this town is capable of" — she swallowed, unable to get out the word *murder*.

Biddle pushed at his sheriff's hat. "We don't know that it's someone from River Bend," he told her. "It could well have been a stranger."

"Please!" Fanny snorted. "Name one person in this town who *didn't* want to kill Milton Grone. I'll wager you can't think of one."

"Fanny," Amos said, disapproving.

"It's true, and you know it."

"Let's take things down a notch, shall we?" Doc's tangled eyebrows knitted as he fixed his wife with a warning glare. "We don't need to stir the pot any further."

Fanny rolled her eyes. "I'd say Milton Grone stirred the pot all by himself."

"Has Shotsie heard?" Helen asked.

"We're on our way to see her," the sheriff said. "I've asked Doc to help me break the news in case she takes it hard." He tugged at his holster, looking decidedly uncomfortable. "I'm afraid she'll get hysterical like she did the other night."

"Of course, Doc should be there," Helen agreed, remembering the distraught woman she'd found crying alone in the kitchen just two days ago. "I can only imagine how upset the whole town's going to be when they get wind of this."

"Murder isn't something we get a lot of in River Bend," the sheriff agreed, turning to face the Grone's house. "But that makes this case a top priority."

Fanny harrumphed. "I wonder if the good citizens of this town won't care much about finding the guilty party at all. They might think he's done us a favor by—"

Abruptly, Doc's wife stopped gabbing.

Helen glanced up at the Grone's front porch and saw exactly what had shut her up or rather *who*.

Shotsie stood with hands on hips, eyeing the group who'd gathered on her lawn. Her hair was a tangled mess and she wore faded jeans, her feet stuffed inside pink slippers. She tugged her oversized cardigan closed, the sleeves hanging down so they nearly obscured her small hands altogether.

"What're you doing in my front yard?" she asked, descending the paint-chipped front steps toward them. "Is there something going on I should know about?"

"Good afternoon, Mrs. Grone," Amos Melville said simply.

"Ma'am," the sheriff mumbled and tugged the beak of his hat.

Shotsie squinted at them as she took a few steps closer. "Why the formality? Spit it out, would you?" she said, then singled out Frank Biddle. "Sheriff, this has to do with Miltie, doesn't it?"

"Yes, ma'am, it does." Biddle took off his hat and began turning it round and round in his hands. "I'm not sure how to put this. Maybe we should go inside," he suggested, but Shotsie would have none of it.

She vigorously shook her head and wailed, "I don't want to go inside! Just say what you have to say then bug off! I'm on my last nerve, and you're stepping on it!"

"Um, Doc, you want to take this?" Biddle asked, swallowing so hard the lump of his Adam's apple jerked.

Amos didn't look any more eager to share the news than the sheriff.

"Would somebody please spill?" Shotsie looked ready to come apart at the seams.

"It's just that I, um, spoke too soon when I initially examined your husband. I, uh, jumped the gun, so to speak," Amos muttered, though the words seemed to trigger a sudden coughing fit. He turned away, wheezing into his hand while Fanny patted his back.

Shotsie's face turned purple. "What's wrong with you people? What's so terrible that you can't even say it? Milton's already dead. What's more awful than that? C'mon, Mrs. Evans, give it to me straight. You're one of the few in this town who doesn't treat me like a leper."

"Well, I . . . hmm." Helen didn't know what to say. She'd only just learned the truth herself. Gazing into Shotsie's weary face, she felt oddly helpless. "It's just that Milton wasn't — well, he didn't have a heart attack," she managed to get out.

Doc's coughing fit subsided, and he touched Helen's arm, letting her off the hook. "The medical examiner's office ran some tests, helping to clarify cause of death."

Shotsie's eyes bugged. "What tests? What could've killed Milt if it wasn't his heart?"

"Lots of other things," Sheriff Biddle said, tucking his hat back on his head.

Shotsie ignored him. "Please, Doc."

Amos put his hand over hers. "The evidence doesn't support a natural death. It appears that Milton was hit on the head. It's the blow that killed him."

"No!" Shotsie backed away, tugging her hand free. "That can't be true. You're telling me Milt was *murdered*?"

"Take it easy, Mrs. Grone," the sheriff said firmly. "I understand how hard this must be for you to digest."

Shotsie's chest heaved. "Hard to digest?" she shrieked. "Are you kidding me? This is crazy! It can't be true, none of it! Murder doesn't happen in a one-horse town like this!"

"It doesn't," Biddle agreed. "Not in the usual scheme of things but anywhere you have people who butt heads there's the potential for viol—"

"Who did it?" Shotsie asked, cutting him off. "Who clobbered my Miltie?"

"I don't know that yet," Biddle told her, rocking back on his heels. "We haven't got much to go on. Only that whatever was used to hit him had some dirt on it. Oh, and fertilizer. The kind used by gardeners."

"Fertilizer?" Shotsie repeated, her round face turning such a mottled shade of purple that Helen thought the woman might pass out. But then, Shotsie reared her head, and Helen saw the wild look that came to her eyes.

Without another word, Shotsie stomped through the high grass toward the split-rail fence, pausing there to stare at something on its other side.

Helen stuck her hands in her jacket pockets. She felt totally unsettled by the turn of events. This latest revelation had hit Shotsie hard, and she'd already had more than enough to endure.

"Fertilizer . . . dirt . . . rust," Shotsie repeated.

Helen went toward her. "C'mon, my dear, let's go inside the house, and I'll make a fresh pot of coffee—"

She hadn't even finished the sentence when Shotsie ducked down, slipping between the fence rails and crashing through the raspberry bushes on the other side.

"Mrs. Grone!" Helen called after her because all she could see beyond the fence was Felicity, still standing on her porch, her wide-brimmed hat seeming enormous atop her thin frame.

"What's she doing?" Biddle said, coming up behind Helen.

But Helen had already sprung into action.

She bent down as Shotsie had, forcing her less agile body through the split rails, and skirted the shrubs that Shotsie had trampled. Calling out, "Mrs. Grone, don't!" she rushed across Felicity's manicured lawn.

Helen didn't stop until she reached the porch steps and paused with her hand on her racing heart, trying hard to catch her breath.

"Mrs. Grone," she called again, but Shotsie didn't turn around.

With her pink slippers set apart, Shotsie cornered Felicity, who'd backed against a porch post. Her hands curled to fists, Shotsie let out a string of curses, her voice raised to megaphone loudness, clear enough for every neighbor to hear within a block.

"I saw you arguing with him that morning," she ranted, "I watched it all from the bedroom window. You shook your watering can at him and looked fit to kill! You hated my Miltie, maybe more than anyone in this Podunk town! I'll bet you did it, you old biddy! Well, *didn't you*?"

"Shotsie, that's enough!" Helen said sharply.

The interruption seemed to throw Shotsie off for a moment.

Enough so that Felicity could scramble around Mrs. Grone, heading for Helen.

With a howl, Shotsie lunged at her, knocking the hat from her head and baring the cropped gray hair.

"Get away from me!" Felicity cried with ashen face and fear-filled eyes. Then she grabbed the shovel she'd leaned near the porch steps and raised it above her shoulder as she faced her attacker.

"Don't come near me," she warned. "Stay away, I said!"

Shotsie screamed, "You did it just like that, didn't you? Took your shovel and *smack*!"

The sheriff brushed past Helen and grabbed Shotsie by the shoulders. "Mrs. Grone, come with me, please, and, you Miss Timmons, put the shovel down."

Felicity glanced over at Helen but she didn't lower the shovel, though it shook in her hands.

Even as the sheriff led her away, Shotsie kept screaming as loud as she could, "You did it! YOU MURDERED MY HUSBAND!"

Felicity swayed, and her fingers lost their grip on the shovel. It fell to the porch steps with a *clang*. Then her eyes rolled up into her head and down she went as well, crumpling up like a ragdoll.

CHAPTER NINETEEN

Helen walked briskly away from Felicity's after having finally gotten her friend to down a cup of chamomile tea along with two Ibuprofen. Felicity was so disturbed by Shotsie's accusations that she'd trembled and wept on and off for nearly an hour. Finally, Helen had calmed her down enough to convince her to lie down.

When Felicity had eventually drifted off, Helen had tucked a blanket around her. Then she slipped out of the house, being careful not to slam the screened door.

She paused at the stone bridge that led to the chapel and looked up at the steeple with its whitewashed clapboard, thinking of Milton's funeral service and all who'd attended it. One among them, she realized, could be his killer.

She shuddered, finding it impossible to believe that Milton had been murdered in cold blood by someone who lived in quiet River Bend.

You did it . . . you murdered my husband!

Shotsie's words to Felicity rattled through her brain, and Helen pressed her fingers to her temples, willing them to go away.

Her friend had not done it, of that Helen felt absolutely sure. Yes, Felicity had lived in fear of Milton, but she could not have harmed the man any more than Helen could have.

But what of Felicity's missing shovel, she suddenly wondered. Could Shotsie be right about one thing at least, that vanishing spade had been used as the murder weapon?

Oh, dear.

Helen sighed. Perhaps it was merely coincidence. Felicity's shovel had likely been swiped by the bored adolescents who rode their bikes up and down the River Road on weekends and invaded River Bend in small packs like prepubescent Hell's Angels.

The squeal of a swing on the nearby playground caught her attention, and Helen turned toward the sound, walking alongside the creek that ran through the chapel's grounds.

She spotted Maddy Fister on the swing, her dark hair limp in her face, her feet listlessly scraping the dirt. She moved to and fro, the motion slow, mournful even, when coupled with the sporadic moan of the chains as they stretched back and forth.

Helen raised a hand to wave, but the girl didn't even look up. She continued to push at ground with the tips of her shoes.

Was it wise for Maddy to be out of bed so soon after she'd miscarried? Helen was tempted to scold her and send her home. But the pastor's daughter looked so sad and lonely, like she needed a hand to hold not a chastising.

Helen crossed the bridge over the creek and entered the playground. Madeline must not have heard her approach as she didn't look up. She kept hanging her head even as Helen said, "Hello, Madeline."

But Maddy just continued her dispirited swaying.

"My, that looks like fun," Helen tried instead. "Why I don't think I've done this since, well, I can't rightly remember." She lowered herself to the swing next to Madeline's. As soon as she pressed her sneakers into the dirt to propel her seat forward, the girl brought her own to a dead stop.

Helen dragged her heels and came to a standstill beside her.

"Maddy, honey," she said, forcing herself to smile despite the girl's frown. "Would you like to talk?"

The girl snorted and stared off in the distance.

"Are you alright? I'm concerned—"

"Don't be 'cause I'm great, okay?" She said it with such anger that Helen was hardly fooled by the declaration. "Can't you just leave me alone?" she muttered and dropped her chin, avoiding Helen's gaze.

"Are you sure you should be up and about so soon?" Helen said softly. "Your body went through something awful."

"Whatever." Madeline rolled her eyes.

"I know you're young and strong, but it might be best not to push it—" Helen stopped herself, biting off the lecture she'd been about to give the girl, deciding that wasn't her place. She wasn't her mother or even her grandma. "Look, you can't blame me for worrying, not after I saw you in such pain. And I know your father's sick over what happened. I wouldn't doubt that he's wondering where you are right now."

"Please." Madeline snapped, her chin jerking up. Her dark eyes crackled with emotion. "My father only worries about himself and how other people see him. He should have minded his own business. He ruined everything for me."

"How do you mean he ruined everything?" Helen held onto the chains and leaned forward, watching Maddy. "Your father didn't cause you to lose the baby. What happened to you was simply . . . life." Helen tried to find an angle maybe a preacher's daughter would better understand. "Perhaps, it was God's plan."

"God's plan?" Madeline repeated and cursed under her breath. "You sound just like him. All I ever hear from his mouth is about what God wants for everyone. What about what I want, huh? Don't I have any say in how I live?"

"I think you must," Helen told her, speaking softly though her tone was firm enough. "If your father had been directing things, I doubt you would have ended up in doc's office, going through such a traumatic experience. That's not what he wanted for you."

Maddy stared at her, her mouth hanging open, as though she couldn't believe Helen had just said what she did. Then she pressed her lips together and started to stand. Only her legs wobbled so much she sat back down again.

"Have you told your boyfriend?" Helen dared to ask.

"My boyfriend?" Maddy laughed.

"Your father said you were involved in a serious relationship, one with an older boy. Is he in college, perhaps?"

"Oh, my God!" The girl turned beet-red. "My dad *told* you that? Can't anything I do in this town be private?"

Helen didn't want Madeline to get the wrong impression so she clarified, "Oh, sweetheart, no, your father didn't spread gossip about you. He was so worried. What he said to me was in the strictest confidence. Besides," Helen went on, "if anyone's given River Bend something to gossip about, it's you. When you're the daughter of a pastor, you're under extra scrutiny, whether you want it or not."

"I don't." Maddy wouldn't look at her.

"Your dad said he nearly called the sheriff. He thought perhaps you were—"

"I wasn't."

"Are you sure?"

Madeline met her eyes and said through gritted teeth, "Why don't you lay off, okay? I have to take enough crap from my dad. I don't need it from someone I'm not even related to."

"Fair enough," Helen said and wiped her hands on her pants. Then she pulled herself up by the swing's chains and stood. "I'll leave you alone if that's what you want." She took one last look at Maddy's angry face and turned away.

"No, wait!"

Helen hesitated.

"You don't have to go," Maddy told her. "You can stay. I mean, it's still mostly a free country."

"Okay," Helen said and returned to the swing. But she didn't talk. She figured it was Maddie's turn to speak.

"Look, Mrs. Evans, it's not you I'm mad at," Madeline said with a sigh. "It's my father."

Helen kept quiet, knowing how difficult it was for the girl to even say that much. She put her hands in her lap and waited.

"I did have, um, something serious going on," she tried to explain, her voice shaky. "But it doesn't matter anymore because it was over almost as fast as it started. My dad saw to that when he found out. You're right that he told the guy he'd report him to the police."

Helen found herself wondering if this "older" guy wasn't a teenager after all. Maybe not even a college kid. Was he a full-grown man, living in River Bend? Helen had seen plenty of promos for Lifetime movies about dads hooking up with the babysitter. If that was the case, it was no wonder the pastor was beside himself.

Maddy blinked to fight back tears. "I thought I was in love, isn't that stupid? Maybe I'm just messed up because I haven't had a mom in so long, and my dad's always busy with everyone else's problems." She stared down at her lap. "It happened over time, slowly. He liked to sit on the rocks by the river, just looking out, like I do sometimes. I saw him there, and we started talking." A vague smile flitted across her lips. "He knew my mom, Mrs. Evans. He said I was a lot like her. That she was kind and pretty, not judgmental like so many folks are."

"It's nice to feel loved," Helen told her, trying to keep the pity from her voice. Lack of self-esteem made young girls so vulnerable, so apt to leap without thinking of the consequences. "Did he know you were pregnant, Maddy?" she asked as kindly as she could. "Did he offer to take responsibility?"

"Take responsibility?" Madeline lifted her chin, and the tears started rolling again, splashing unheeded down her cheeks. "He was married."

The girl's lover was older *and* married?

Oh, boy.

Helen grabbed the chains on her either side to keep from falling off her seat. She did her best to keep her shock to herself. And, because Maddy didn't answer her question, she asked again, "Did he know about the baby?"

Madeline nodded. "I thought he'd be glad, that it'd give him a reason to leave his wife. I'm eighteen next month. I could have put off college and done virtual courses, whatever it took. We could have gotten married if he'd wanted to. Only, he didn't."

The girl paused for a moment, sniffling, and Helen reached for her hand. She half-expected Madeline to pull away but she didn't.

"I thought he loved me," she whispered, "that he wanted to take care of me. I told myself he'd change his mind if I gave him some space. But it doesn't matter now anyway. It's too late."

Helen sighed. What a mess! She wished she could get the fellow's name and go wring his neck. Why would a grown man do this to such a fragile child? What could he have been thinking? If Helen had been in Earnest Fister's shoes, she would have called the police and had the son of a gun arrested, for sure.

But the pastor had backed down, because Madeline had asked him to. He was so afraid of losing her, of letting her down.

What a terrible pickle.

She squeezed Madeline's hand. "I know this sounds ridiculous at the moment when everything's so painful, but maybe it's for the best. I truly believe things happen for a reason."

The girl stiffened. "That's what my father said."

"He loves you so much, you know," Helen told her. "Maybe you should listen to him now and then."

"No, thanks." Madeline slipped her hand free of Helen's and stood so abruptly the chains on the swing rattled. "My father messed things up for me, and I'll blame him for that till the day I die. I swear I will!"

Then she took off running.

Helen could hear her sobs as she crossed the playground and raced over the bridge.

What had just happened?

What was happening to River Bend?

First, Milton Grone's death that had turned into murder and now Madeline Fister admitting to having had an affair with an older, married man.

Helen sighed, thinking that her cozy hometown had suddenly come to resemble a real-life soap opera with way more drama than any of them had bargained for.

CHAPTER TWENTY

When Helen arrived back at her own doorstep, she found the screened door ajar, just enough space between it and the jamb for a twenty-pound cat to slip through.

Her yellow tom had left another sign of his comings and goings as well: smack in the center of the porch lay a lifeless gray bird. Helen prayed he was a bachelor and not a momma with a nest full of babies waiting for her return.

"Oh, Amber," she said with a shake of her head. If only she could keep him inside! But she and Joe had tried for years, and it just didn't stick. Maybe Amber had been feral too long to adjust.

She stepped carefully around the feathered corpse and went to the kitchen to fetch a paper sack and a piece of cardboard. Then she returned to the porch to dispose of the little "gift" her fur-child had left her.

Afterward, she sought out Amber and found him in her bedroom, curled atop her flowered spread. He was sleeping so peacefully — belly up, paws in the air, a pink-gummed smile on his mouth — that she didn't have the heart to disturb him in order to give him another talking to.

Back in the kitchen, she scrubbed her hands at the sink before fixing a glass of iced tea. She took it with her to the porch and settled in her wicker rocker, picking up the crossword she hadn't quite finished earlier in the day.

She'd barely gotten her purple pen uncapped, when a voice called to her from beyond the screens.

"Yoo-hoo!" someone chirped. "Helen, are you there?"

Grudgingly, she set aside the paper and stood. At the door stood Clara Foley in a blinding orange muumuu.

"Oh, good! You're home," Clara said, doing a happy little wiggle.

"I only just got back," Helen told her, making no move to invite her in. If she did, Clara would plunk down on the sofa, wanting to gossip away the afternoon. But Helen was in no mood to chat about the latest scuttlebutt.

"So have you heard?" Clara asked, her nose pressed to the screen.

"That depends," Helen said. There was too much going on in River Bend these days to have heard everything.

"If I don't share, I'll swear, I'll burst," Clara said, snatching open the door before Helen could do it herself. Once inside, Clara grabbed her arm. "It's about Milton Grone," she leaned nearer to whisper. "It was no heart attack that killed him."

"No," Helen said, feigning surprise.

"Get this." Clara cupped a hand to the side of her mouth and hissed, "Someone bashed in his head."

"I can't believe it," Helen replied, which wasn't a lie. She hadn't yet had the chance to fully digest that bit of news.

Clara's chin wobbled as she nodded. "Even worse is that Shotsie Grone practically announced to the world that she thinks Felicity Timmons is guilty."

Helen's face warmed, and she felt every bit as angry as she had when she'd witnessed Mrs. Grone hurl the accusation. "That's absurd," she scoffed. "Felicity wouldn't hurt a fly, and you know it."

"Oh, honey, I'm with you," Clara agreed. "But try to convince the Widow Grone of it. She's been ranting and raving that Felicity's the culprit ever since she found out that her husband was murdered."

"Well, she's wrong," Helen said, not wanting to hear any more. She nudged Clara toward the door. "If you wouldn't mind, I have things to do."

"But don't you want to know the rest?" Clara said, grabbing the door frame before Helen could shove her out.

There was more?

"They found it!" Clara squealed, her eyes twin pins of light.

Helen sighed. "Found what?"

"The murder weapon, of course!" Clara clapped her hands together like an excited child. "The sheriff searched the woods behind Felicity's place and nearly tripped over an old shovel lying in the brush. I heard there was blood all over it."

Helen lost her breath for a moment.

"Are you all right, Hel? You look pale."

Dear God. Helen's heart pumped frantically. She had a bad feeling about this, a horrible feeling.

"I've got to go," she announced, pushing past her friend.

She only made it as far as her stoop.

"Now hold on!" Clara caught her arm from behind. "If you're headed to Felicity's, she isn't there."

Helen froze.

"Sheriff Biddle took her down to his office for questioning."

"What?"

"He drove her there himself in the squad car."

Helen groaned, wondering how things could possibly get any worse.

* * *

Five minutes later, Helen stood at the door of the one-man sheriff's department in the heart of Main Street. The tiny station house sat between LaVryle's Cut 'n' Curl and a dusty antiques store. Helen went inside to find herself in a room whose walls were papered with the faces of Illinois' Most Wanted as well as hand-printed cards inquiring about lost pets and advertising garage sales.

"What's going on here?" she said as Biddle rose from behind his desk.

Felicity spun around in the chair opposite his. "Oh, Helen!" she said, looking fit to cry. She didn't even have a hat on, which was a rare sight indeed. Her sparse gray hair appeared matted as though Biddle had snatched her up from a nap, which he probably had.

Helen marched over to her dear friend straightaway, glaring at the sheriff. "Frank Biddle, have you lost your mind?"

"Just a danged minute, Mrs. Evans," Biddle replied, puffing out his chest. "I'm not booking Miss Timmons, I'm only asking her some questions. You probably don't know as yet, but I found a shovel in the woods behind her house. It was covered with—"

"Blood," Helen finished for him. "Yes, I heard." She glanced down at Felicity, who'd sunk back into the chair. "That doesn't mean Felicity hid the shovel much less used it to kill Milton Grone."

"Like I was saying," Biddle went on, huffily, "Miss Timmons is not being arrested for murder. But I had to bring her in what with Mrs. Grone hollering her head off about it. How would it have looked if I hadn't brought Miss Timmons in at all?"

"Of course," Helen said.

Biddle cleared his throat. "Doc Melville thinks it might well be the murder weapon. There was dirt and rust on it, plus plant fertilizer, like in the medical examiner's report. Doc's getting it checked out as we speak. We'll know the truth before long."

The truth, Helen thought, seemed more and more elusive all the time.

"So, are you finished here then? Is Felicity free to go?" Helen asked. "I hardly think you can hold her here without any solid evidence."

"Just a few more questions, please, ma'am," Biddle said. He stared across the desk at Felicity, looking for confirmation.

Helen opened her mouth to protest but Felicity gave a weak nod, and the sheriff plopped down into his chair.

He clicked the ballpoint of his pen, which he held poised to write. "Before we were interrupted" — he glanced at Helen — "I was about to ask if you had a heated argument with Milton Grone the morning of his death?"

Felicity's answer was a meek, "Yes, I argued with him."

"Can you tell me what the fight was about?"

Felicity's hands smoothed her wrinkled housedress. "It was about his fence," she said, her voice soft but sure. "He built it six inches onto my property, which he knew bloody well." She glanced up at the sheriff. "It was a sore spot, but certainly not worth killing him over. I'd already had Art Beaner come see for himself, and he promised he'd take up the matter at the town meeting."

The meeting last Thursday, Helen thought, when the whole town hall had emptied and lit out for Milton's house.

Biddle finished jotting down notes on his legal pad then tapped the pen against his jaw. "Did you have your shovel with you that morning, ma'am?"

"I did, yes," Felicity told him, leaning forward, hands on her knees. "But that's only because I'd just planted new raspberry bushes. I left the shovel outside near the fence, and I didn't remember to fetch it until much later, well after dark." She turned to glance at Helen. There was raw fear in her eyes. "After they'd already found Mr. Grone lying dead in his yard."

"She's telling the truth, Sheriff," Helen said, jumping in. "I saw Felicity pick up her shovel and move it. Why would she have left it out if she'd been the one to kill Grone with it? That would have been really stupid."

"Thanks for your input, Mrs. Evans." Biddle gave her a look but didn't write anything down. He turned his attention back to Felicity. "What happened to the shovel after you moved it, Miss Timmons?"

Felicity's shoulders sagged. "My heavens, Sheriff, I didn't bother with the shovel again until this afternoon. I'd been so gobsmacked by the turn of events that I realized I hadn't cleaned my gardening tools properly. So, I gathered them up to wash. I did the trowels first. But the shovel, well." She put her hands to her cheeks and shook her head. "It had simply disappeared."

"Disappeared?" Biddle wrinkled his brow.

"It was just gone," Felicity said. "I couldn't find it anywhere."

"And you didn't see it again until I recovered it from the brush behind your house half an hour ago?"

"I didn't hide my shovel in the woods." Felicity sounded on the verge of tears. "I didn't know it was there, Sheriff, I swear."

"Enough," Helen said and stepped in front of Felicity, turning her back to the sheriff at his desk. "She's told you all there is to tell," she added, taking hold of Felicity hands and helping her up.

Biddle jumped up on his boots and waved his pen at Helen. "Whoa there, Mrs. Evans, this isn't up to you—"

"Good day, Sheriff," Helen interrupted, guiding Felicity toward the door.

She ignored Frank Biddle's sputtered cries of indignation, thinking he was in over his head. How in God's name did he imagine he was going to track down Milton's murderer if he spent all his time interviewing the likes of Felicity Timmons?

Or had he already made up his mind that poor Felicity was the killer?

CHAPTER TWENTY-ONE

By dinner-time that Sunday night, all of River Bend had heard the news that Milton Grone had been clubbed to death with a bloody shovel belonging to Felicity Timmons.

The 91-year-old mayor of River Bend — whose chronic gout mostly kept him homebound — even shuffled over to Main Street to pay Biddle a visit. He'd popped in both his hearing aids before asking the sheriff if he'd "collared the varmint whodunit."

Since the scene of the crime had been pretty well trampled by half the town last Thursday evening, Biddle didn't have much to go on except Doc's lab tests and the accusations of Milton's widow.

Since Shotsie had seen Milt before leaving for the town meeting at seven and his lifeless body had been found a few minutes before eight o'clock, Biddle estimated the time of death somewhere in between.

That was the easy part.

As Milton's most vocal enemies had been present at town hall and could testify to each other's whereabouts, the sheriff faced an almost impossible task. He was tempted to use the Eenie Meenie Miney Mo method and randomly pick someone to arrest.

"You're a smart man, Frank," Sarah had told him when she'd dropped off fried chicken and biscuits. "You'll figure it out."

Frank forged ahead, drawing up a list of those who'd had the biggest beef with Milton. One-by-one, he'd haul them in for questioning, starting bright and early the next morning.

The first name that he wrote was Felicity Timmons. He put a checkmark beside it since he'd already grilled her.

The next two on his list were Ida Bell and Dorothy Feeny. They'd hardly kept their feelings for Grone a secret. Ida had even gone so far as to call Milton "a murderer" in the newspaper, saying he didn't deserve to live if he let the water park drive countless critters out of their homes.

Biddle paused for a moment, gnawing the inside of his cheek while he pondered who should follow. How about Art Beaner and the whole darned board of directors? All of them had been fighting with Grone ever since the man had moved into his parents' house across from Felicity. Frank recalled an instance when Beaner showed up at the station, red-faced and out of breath. He'd gone to see Grone about association fees past due, and Milton had greeted him with a badly-aimed pop from his shotgun.

Then there was Delilah Grone, Milton's first wife. Biddle had heard the rumors about the woman going after Grone for unpaid alimony and child support. Maybe she figured it'd be easier to get her claws on Milton's water-park windfall if he were dead rather than alive.

Last but not least, Biddle jotted down the name: Shotsie Grone. She'd been acting the part of the grieving widow well enough, and he wasn't sure anyone could put on a show like that without really feeling it inside. But Frank knew from his years in law enforcement that it was more often the spouse who did it than the butler.

Besides, he mused, women were more than a little unpredictable, especially when that time of the month rolled around. Though Sarah would have his head if she knew he were even thinking such a thing. "Mansplaining," she'd call it.

Finished with his list, Biddle slipped it into a folder and set it aside. Then he snatched up his hat and stepped out of the office just as the chapel's prized carillon began to chime, "Sweet Adelaide."

He got in his car and drove the three blocks to Doc Melville's. Within minutes, he'd parked at the curb in front of the A-frame painted red as a barn. He avoided the front door, going around to the side entrance that led into Doc's office. He stood on the welcome mat beneath the old-fashioned shingle that neatly proclaimed, "Amos Melville, M.D.," and he doffed his hat. Then he turned the knob and went inside.

"Hey, Doc, it's me, Frank Biddle," he called out as he walked into the empty waiting area. The front desk, usually manned by Fanny, was deserted.

"Amos?" he said again, heading up the hallway past an empty exam room.

Yellow light streamed from an opened door toward the rear. That, Biddle knew, was where Amos kept his lab.

He tucked his hat atop his head and hiked up his pants before knocking on the door frame. "Yo, Doc," he said, seeing Amos hunched over a table. "Am I interrupting?"

"Ah, hello, Sheriff." Amos glanced briefly up from the item sprawled across the stainless-steel surface. It was the shovel Frank had found behind Miss Timmons's house. "I was just finishing up," Doc said, and Frank nodded, hanging back in the doorway.

"What'd you find?" he asked.

"I typed the blood on the shovel, and it's 0-positive," Doc told him. "That's the same type as Milton Grone. I'll have Ed Drake's office run a DNA test, of course. I don't have the means to do that here." The doctor sighed and scratched his chin with the back of a latex-gloved hand. "My gut tells me that'll show a match to Grone as well."

Biddle got tired of standing and pulled up an empty stool. "Did you find anything else, something that would point to who hit him?"

In response, Amos turned the tool upside-down so that the backside of the spade could be viewed. He stooped over it, his spectacled eyes hovering above a spot an inch below. He poked at something with a metal stick that looked like a dental pick. "You see that?" the doc asked.

Biddle leaned forward. "It looks like little flecks of rock and, I dunno, dirt and stuff."

Amos pointed the metal stick at Frank's "flecks of rock," explaining, "that's bone from Milton's shattered temporal lobe. Someone whacked him awfully hard. In a fit of rage, I'd wager."

Frank felt his stomach lurch and tasted the fried chicken he'd eaten not a half hour earlier. He swallowed before finding his voice again. "Do you figure Felicity Timmons had the strength to clobber Grone with enough force to kill him? She's, what, seventy-five if she's a day."

Amos met the sheriff's gaze. "If you're asking me if I believe Felicity could've murdered a man, the answer is no."

Biddle shifted on his feet. "That's your personal opinion, Doc," he said. "What's your professional opinion?"

"She didn't do it, Frank," Amos said, shaking his head. "You're fishing in the wrong barrel."

"Her prints are on the handle."

The doctor harrumphed. "Why wouldn't her prints be on the handle? It's her shovel. She's not denying it. Will you put her in jail for that?"

Biddle slid off the stool and headed for the door. There, he paused. "You're not making this any easier on me, Doc."

"Nothing about this situation is easy," Amos said and began to peel off his gloves. "Isn't there a part of you that wants to just let this one go?"

Even if there was — even if he wanted to — Biddle couldn't do that.

He shook his head.

"That's what I thought," Amos replied and patted Frank's shoulder before he flipped off the light and left the room.

The sheriff stood in the dark for a while after, trying to think of when he'd last had to deal with a crime as serious as this. He'd come to River Bend from a city police force when the tiny town had advertised for a new sheriff. He'd run for the office unopposed and had kept the gig for nearly fifteen years. Not once in all that time had there been a murder.

Though there had been one other dead body.

A corpse had been found floating in the harbor two summers ago. But it wasn't the victim of a crime. Heck, it wasn't even human. The floater had been Homer Brown's geriatric German shepherd. As best as he could surmise, the dog had been chasing a muskrat, had plunged into the muddy water, and had been unable to get out.

If only this case were as simple to put away.

Biddle glanced through the dim at the shovel in Doc's lab and wondered what skeletons it would unearth if only it could talk.

CHAPTER TWENTY-TWO

At half past seven on Monday morning, Helen had fed the cat, dressed in a navy-blue sweatsuit, and double-knotted the laces on her size six sneakers.

She'd been too preoccupied lately to take her usual two-mile walk to the river and back so she made it a point to do just that. Not only would it give her heart and lungs a good work-out, but it would give her time to think besides.

It was still early enough that the town was quiet, and Helen strolled past sleepy block after block, feeling as if she was alone in the world. Houses appeared to slumber; window shades drawn like closed eyelids. The sun peeked at her in sporadic bursts of light from beyond the surrounding bluffs. In the treetops overhead, birds began to arise, chirruping like hyperactive coo-coo clocks.

Her mind was not on their cheery songs, though. Instead, her attention drifted, as it always did these days, to the death of Milton Grone. She found it hard to dwell on anything else when that was all everyone in town seemed to talk about, each one trying guess who did it and wondering if the killer could be living right next door.

It shook Helen to realize that such a hideous crime had occurred so close to home. She knew the world was changing around her, that drugs were as commonplace in small towns as big cities, and guns were bought, sold, and stolen like trading cards. But River Bend had always seemed far removed from the sort of everyday crime that plagued nearby Alton, just a twenty-minute ride down the River Road, or St. Louis City, less than an hour away.

Helen had always felt so secure in this place. Why, she and Joe hadn't had locks installed on the house until sometime in the seventies, when the last of their four kids had gotten out of college and moved away. Half the time, Helen forgot to secure the doors, and, despite living alone, she had never felt the least afraid.

Until the murder of Milton Grone.

She glanced around her, to her right and left, quickening her pace.

When she realized what she'd done, she laughed at herself, though the pitch of it sounded far too high. Even she wasn't fooled by her poor attempt at bravado.

She slowed her steps, telling herself Sheriff Biddle would find the killer soon enough.

Only that, too, caused her worry.

You murdered my husband!

Shotsie's words rang in her ears, and she frowned, angry at the woman for pointing a finger at Felicity. Milton's widow certainly had some nerve! And Frank Biddle himself, why he was no better, hauling Felicity down to his office in his squad car because of the whims of a hysterical widow.

Yes, Felicity's shovel had been used as the murder weapon but that hardly meant the old girl did the deed. Why, anyone could have accessed the spade. Everyone knew that Felicity kept her gardening tools out back. On that Thursday night when Milton died, any one of a number of townsfolk could have crept into Felicity's yard in the dark, picked up the shovel, smacked Milton upside the head, then returned it to Felicity's as if nothing had happened.

Even I could have done it, Helen concluded as she approached the town hall, eyeing its quaint whitewashed brick and black trim. But she hadn't and neither had Felicity, she concluded as she passed the building and moved on.

Half a dozen other residents of River Bend had better reasons to want Milton dead than a disagreement over a split-rail fence. Ida and Dot had been publicly fighting Grone tooth and nail since the sale of that land on the riverfront. Art Beaner and the town board had disputes over unpaid community fees going back at least a decade.

Still, Helen had a hard time convincing herself that any one of them had actually bludgeoned the bastard.

With a sigh, she pressed on past the playground, approaching the chapel.

When it came right down to it, she figured, the killer had done the town a favor. Even as she thought it, she realized how horrid it sounded. But from her perch, folks seemed as relieved at Milton's death as they appeared disbelieving that such a crime had actually happened. In fact, she'd even heard someone murmuring to his breakfast companion at the diner the other morning that Milton's death was a most convenient murder.

Now Grone's neighbors could live in peace and Art Beaner's board had been rid of the thorn in its side. Even Ida and Dot had one less obstacle to battle in their war against the water park.

The growl of an engine suddenly and loudly invaded the quiet of the morning, interrupting Helen's thoughts.

With a whoosh of gravel and dust, a van whipped past her, tearing up the road toward the river. Helen turned away until the gritty air had settled. Coughing the rest out of her lungs, she shook her head, having recognized the truck that delivered the morning's *Telegraph*.

Did he think he was Jeff Gordon careening around the track in a NASCAR race? She fumed as she brushed herself off.

"Mrs. Evans!"

The voice startled her no less than the speeding van and she spun about, hand to heart, seeing Earnest Fister hurrying toward her.

Clad in black trousers and white button-down shirt, he took the chapel's steps two by two, striding forward in an agile sprint. He crossed the stone bridge in a blink and was quickly at her side.

"Are you alright?" he asked. "That paper boy's going to run down someone one of these days."

"I'm fine," she told him, and she was. She held her palms apart by several feet, much as a fisherman bragging of his latest catch. "He missed me by this much."

Fister's brooding features didn't relax one iota. His dark eyes looked to the road as he told her, "I've called the paper myself to complain about his driving, but they don't seem particularly concerned."

Helen smiled. "They're probably glad to have anyone at all willing to do the job this far out of Alton and with the sun barely up. Speaking of which" — she hooked a thumb toward the chapel. "What's got you working at the crack of dawn on a Monday? Is the town so full of sinners you've resorted to putting in overtime?"

The expression that crossed the clergyman's face was something other than amusement. His mouth pulled taut. "I came to be alone," he murmured. "It's difficult for me to think at home, what with Madeline moping about and glaring at me. I have more privacy here besides."

"I see." Helen knew from her chat with Madeline Fister the day before that the girl blamed her father for all her recent troubles. She felt nearly as sorry for the pastor as for Maddie. "How is she?"

"She's healing," Fister said without much conviction so that Helen wondered if the opposite wasn't true.

"She certainly has a lot to deal with for someone her age, doesn't she?" Helen glanced at him sideways. "I have to wonder how on earth she became involved with a married man," she went on, before she could catch herself.

Fister's dark eyes turned on Helen with an intensity that made Helen take a step back. "She told you that?"

Helen swallowed hard. "I'm sorry if I spoke out of turn," she got out. "But Madeline brought that up herself," she explained, wondering if he thought she'd heard something on the town grapevine. "Perhaps she said it just to shock me."

The minister didn't reply. He simply stared at her.

Instead of clamming up, as she probably should have, Helen nervously babbled on. "She said she'd thought he'd loved her, that she'd had hopes he'd leave his wife . . ."

Fister laughed so abruptly it made Helen jump. "She was a fool," he said, shaking his head. "But I don't blame her. She's young and naive and without a mother's hand to guide her. He saw her weakness and preyed on it. No matter how she wants to see it, he took advantage of her," he said through gritted teeth. "He was a grown man. He should've known better." He stopped and looked at the sky as the pinks and grays of sunrise changed chameleon-like to blue. "He had no right," Fister whispered, still staring above. "He had no right."

Helen reached out to touch his arm, and he started, as if he'd forgotten she was there. "Don't blame yourself," she told him. "You did not push her into his arms, despite what Maddy thinks."

"Blame myself?"

"I can hear the guilt in your voice."

He took a step away, pressing his palms together, and Helen realized suddenly that there was more to all of this than what she knew. "If you hear guilt in my voice, it's not for anything I've done. It's for waiting as long as I did to do anything at all," he told her, though he didn't meet her eyes. "You must understand there was no other way. My fears were for Madeline, for what he'd do to her, what he'd already he'd done." Fister raised fists to the heavens. "By God, he put her through hell." With a sigh, his broad shoulders lost their stiffness. "At least now he won't bother her again."

"Of course, he won't," Helen echoed, certain that was what he wanted to hear. She hoped that, both for his sake and Madeline's, it was the truth. "He's out of her life, and she'll get on as before. She's young and, from what I've seen, quite resilient. She'll be over this before you know it."

He dropped his hands to his sides and shook his head. "I'm not sure she'll ever forgive me."

"She loves you."

"Does she?"

"She's your child, your flesh and blood," Helen reminded him.

A wry smile took shape on his mouth as he told her, "I don't know if that matters to her anymore. Not this time."

Helen wondered what it was he wasn't saying for she could see there was something more he was holding back, something that was eating at him inside. "It must be hard for you, watching your child become a young woman."

"Maybe she wouldn't have gone looking for trouble if her mother were alive."

"I'm sure you did your best," Helen said. "It's all any of us can do. Raising children isn't easy. They have minds of their own, and they grow up far too quickly these days."

His brow wrinkled. "But it's my duty to teach right from wrong, and I clearly failed."

"Well, she confided in you, didn't she?" Helen said, wishing he could see that it wasn't so hopeless after all. "Isn't that how you found out about her relationship?"

"No," he said, gazing off again.

"You don't mean to say that the man she was involved with—" Helen let the question hang, noticing the deep flush that rose from Fister's neck.

The minister didn't remark one way or the other. He stared past her, arms folded across his chest. His bearded face looked grim.

So that was what had happened, Helen knew then without a doubt. Maddy's married lover had confronted the minister. Perhaps it had been a confession of sorts? Or, she wondered, was it a taunt?

"Would you like to talk about it?" she said since the can of worms had already been opened.

"I think it's time I returned to my desk," he said briskly, nodding at her. "Good day, Mrs. Evans." He walked away, leaving her standing on the sidewalk.

She watched him cross the bridge and ascend the steps to the chapel in no time. He briefly glanced at her from the doorway before he ducked inside.

"Well, for heaven's sake," she said aloud and tried to piece together her conversation with Madeline yesterday and her words with the pastor this morning.

She furrowed her brow.

Who was this older, married man who'd taken advantage of a young girl and told the pastor about the affair himself? Fister said the affair was done, and the despicable fellow would never, ever bother Maddy again.

Oh, my.

Helen's eyes went wide.

Was it possible, she wondered, could it truly be?

A crow squawked at her from the telephone wires above her, and Helen shook away the crazy idea that had popped into her head.

"Absurd," she muttered and, with once last look at the church, picked up her walk where she'd left off.

CHAPTER TWENTY-THREE

After she'd gone to the river and turned back, Helen made a point of stopping at Felicity's. She found the old girl out front in her yard. Down on all fours, Felicity was plucking weeds from a petunia bed. She chattered on all the while, coaxing the flowers to "grow up pretty for Mummy."

Helen smiled, recalling that even Prince Charles had been observed nattering to his plants. And Helen wasn't embarrassed to admit that she conversed with Amber as though the cat understood her every word.

"Good morning," she said as she approached.

Felicity looked up. "Oh, hello!" she said and scrambled to her feet. "I thought I'd get an early start. It's so much cooler in the hour after daybreak," she explained as she tugged off her gloves then brushed at dirty knees.

"I hope I'm not interrupting," Helen said because she hadn't meant for Felicity to stop her work just to chat.

"No, no." Felicity adjusted the brim of her straw hat and linked her arm through Helen's. "In fact, I'm glad you came by. I picked some blackberries earlier, and I've got a pint for you."

"What a dear!" Helen patted her hand. "It's sweet of you to think of me."

"I find if I stay busy, I'm less likely to think of" — She swallowed and squeaked out, "Everything."

Helen noticed the hollows beneath her usually vivid eyes as Felicity's gaze shifted toward the fence.

"Oh, hon, please, don't fret," Helen said, wishing she could offer some real words of comfort. "It'll all be over with soon, I'm sure, and then life will get back to normal. Mark my words."

Felicity sighed. She usually had such good posture with shoulders straight and chin up, but now she seemed just to slump. She attempted a smile but it was feeble at best. "You're right, of course. It's not like me to be so bloody spineless."

"I'd never call you spineless," Helen insisted. "Why you've more gumption than the Queen, may she rest in peace."

Felicity blushed.

"Now where are those delectable blackberries?"

"If you'd like to come inside, I'll fetch them for you," Felicity said then made the mistake of glancing over at the Grones' house yet again. She would have stumbled had Helen not caught her arm. A tiny whimper escaped her throat, and Helen looked across the fence to find the cause of her distress.

There in the window stood Shotsie Grone. Her blond hair made a frizzy aureole around her face as she stared brazenly at them. Though the screen turned her features bleary, her scowl was visible enough.

Then her hand jerked down the shade and she was gone.

"Oh, my, I thought I was done with that lot, but I guess I'm not, am I?" Felicity mumbled, swaying ever-so-slightly.

"It's all right," Helen said, hoping her friend wouldn't faint.

"She as wicked as he was," Felicity whispered.

Helen opened her mouth to deny it, to explain that Shotsie was just distraught and misguided. But she knew none of that would help. The Grones had caused Felicity immeasurably pain, and even the most stalwart of souls could only take so much.

"Come on," she urged, leading her friend toward the lovely white Victorian with its intricate gingerbread trim. "Let's go inside and have some tea, okay?"

At Felicity's nod, Helen walked alongside her into the house and to the sunny kitchen. She settled her friend into a seat at the polished oak table. Kitty, Felicity's tabby-cat, glanced up from a window sill to blink at them, before settling back to sleep post-yawn. Helen figured that dear old Kitty didn't pine for Milton Grone and his shotgun any more than her owner.

Whistling tunelessly, Helen busied herself filling the teapot and setting it on the stove to boil. She gathered up two china cups and saucers from the cabinet, found the strainer and a tin of loose Earl Grey, and lined up everything on the tiled countertop.

"Don't let Shotsie get you so worked up," she said when Felicity sighed overloudly. "You'll drive yourself mad if you do."

"I know, I know," Felicity murmured and raised trembling hands to unpin her hat from her crown. "It's just that always seems to be watching. I feel her eyes on me all the time. Even in my dreams. I barely slept a wink." She set the straw hat aside and dropped her hands to her lap. "I've been hearing voices in the middle of the night," she quietly admitted, "people arguing and a loud popping noise, like a gun."

"It's probably someone's TV turned too loud or your imagination working overtime," Helen told her, unearthing a box of butter cookies and bringing a plate of them to the table.

"True," Felicity agreed. "But I'm a dreadful wreck regardless and all because of him."

Helen picked up a cookie. "What's done is done," she said. "No matter who killed Milton, he won't ever be back. Shotsie told me she's not staying on once everything's settled, so soon you'll be rid of her, too."

Felicity picked at a cookie. "You don't believe I did it, do you?"

"What?" Helen had taken a nibble of a cookie and bit her tongue instead. She flinched at the pain as much as the question, "For goodness' sake, of course, I don't think you killed Milton."

"But the shovel was mine."

"You'd left it outside. Anyone could have used it."

"But I had a good reason. I hated him enough to do it."

Helen didn't like seeing her friend like this. "Stop this! You're innocent."

"Shotsie doesn't believe that," Felicity went on, "and I'm not so sure about the sheriff."

The teapot whistled, and Helen jumped up to fetch it. She strained the tea and poured it into Felicity's favorite sterling server then collected the cream, spoons, and china on a tray and took it all to the table.

"You've got to forget what Shotsie said," Helen insisted as she poured them each a steaming cup. "She's pretty irrational right now."

Felicity blew on her tea, saying nothing.

Helen leaned in. "The local grapevine is painting you as something a hero."

"Pish posh," Felicity said but perked up. "What do the gossips say about the murder? Do you imagine Biddle will find the culprit soon?"

Helen took her friend's hand and held it tight. No doubt Felicity was as unnerved by the goings-on as Helen. They'd once felt secure in their own homes only to have Milton's murder take that away from them. "Frank Biddle might be a bit of a so-and-so, but he'll figure this out," Helen said, reassuring herself as much as Felicity.

"And until he does," her friend added in a quiet voice, "we'll just all have to stay on our toes."

Helen found her gaze drifting over to the window where Kitty lay. Beyond the glass, she had a clear view of the split-rail fence and the patch of unkempt grass where they'd found Milton.

Someone had deliberately set the dead man's head upon a rock to give the impression that the gash was caused after he fell, not before. No stranger wandering into town would have felt the need to cover up the crime. And whoever struck the death blow had to be someone who knew that Milton had a history of heart troubles, like his father.

Much as Helen wished to believe that no one in River Bend could have acted with such violence, the facts didn't lie.

She picked up her teacup, the brew hot enough to burn her tongue. Even so, it didn't rid her of the chill she felt in knowing that a killer lived among them.

CHAPTER TWENTY-FOUR

"Why, Sheriff, you know good and well where we were on Thursday night," Ida Bell scoffed. "We were at the town meeting as Art Beaner can attest."

"Yes, that's exactly where we were," Dot Feeny piped up and bobbed her head.

The sheriff eyed the women from behind the safety of his desk. "And you said you arrived when exactly?"

"We were practically the first ones there," Dot told him, glancing sideways at Ida as if seeking approval. "Sat right in front, we did."

Ida tapped a mud-splattered boot against the floor. "Everyone in town hall saw us," she stated, adding gruffly, "I reminded them all of what a horrid thing this water-park deal is, and I didn't mince words."

"No, she didn't mince anything, Sheriff, I promise," Dot remarked.

"Oh, I don't doubt that," Frank told her and pretended to scribble while surreptitiously studying the pair perched on chairs across from him. Ida looked remarkably like a long-legged crane and Dot, a more compact hoot owl; each of them taking turns squawking at him.

"Do you honestly think I murdered Milton Grone?" Ida asked with a sniff. "I'm not afraid to confess that I didn't like him, Sheriff. No, I didn't like him at all." Ida's angular features settled in an impatient frown. "Hell's bells, but he had zero concern for the environment. His idea of recycling was tossing soda pop cans to the side of the road, so that someone else could come along and pick them up." She clamped her teeth together and ground out, "He was a greedy, unconscionable son of a . . ."

"Gun," Dot said before Ida could spit out another word.

Ida ignored her. "I can't tell you in good conscience that I've shed a single tear over his passing," she went on. "I'm sure I'm not alone. I doubt the grocer's sold out of tissues. Nope. No one's crying over Milton Grone." She gave a toss of her head and declared, "The world's a far better place without him."

"Just because she despised him, doesn't mean anything," Dot said and hunched her round shoulders. "Ida can't stand to see any animal slaughtered."

"Oh?" Frank lifted his pen from the page — and his eyebrows as well — at that one.

"What I meant, of course, is that Ida's a protector of all species," Dot clarified, her cheeks flushed. "She's not a killer."

Ida slapped a skinny thigh. "Dad-gummit, Biddle! If I'd wanted to exterminate Milton Grone, I would have done it long ago, before he finalized that deal with the lowlifes at Wet 'n' Woolly!"

"Yes, she would have done it long ago," Dot chimed in, causing Ida to roll her eyes.

"Look, you two." Frank set down his pen and rubbed his jaw. "I'm not accusing anyone of anything. I'm just trying to put together the pieces."

"Surely you have a lead in the case?" Ida pressed him, bemusement on her flinty face. "You've found fingerprints certainly? Foot tracks in the dirt?"

"I'm working on it," Frank replied and glanced down at his pathetic scribbles. He felt his neck grow warm, and he shuffled papers on his desk, feeling more irritated by the moment. He *had* found fingerprints on the shovel, yes, but they didn't tell him anything he didn't know.

As for tracks in the dirt . . . well, Frank hadn't even realized a crime had been committed until they'd already held the funeral service for Milton. By then, several days had passed and the crime scene was a trampled mess, any evidence destroyed by moving the body. But Doc had assumed that Grone had died of natural causes. They'd had no reason to treat the case as murder, not then.

Once evidence had shown otherwise there wasn't much of anything left to find. So, the sheriff had little to go on except Felicity Timmons' shovel and the fact that Miss Timmons and Milton Grone had argued the morning of the murder.

Frank pressed at his temples, feeling a headache coming on.

"Do you have a prime suspect?" Ida barked, and he glanced up. "Other than Felicity, of course, as everyone knows she didn't do it."

"I'm pursuing leads." The sheriff closed his eyes, willing the headache — and the two women — to go away.

Ida Bell harrumphed, and Biddle opened his eyes to see her sitting with bony elbows braced upon turned-in knees. Her long neck was stretched forward in a manner reminiscent of Canadian geese. "You don't have squat yet, do you?" she said.

Frank squirmed, thinking he was the one who was supposed to be doing the questioning. "I haven't uncovered enough to put anyone under arrest."

"I see." Ida looked sideways at Dotty, and her thin lips curved enigmatically. "Don't beat yourself up if you can't figure out who did it. Whoever axed Milton Grone deserves a medal not jail-time in my humble opinion."

"Axed?" Frank stared at her.

"She meant shoveled," Dot corrected. "Ida sometimes goes for hyperbole."

Oh, really? Frank wanted to stab himself in both eyes with his pen.

"May we go now?" Ida scuffed her boots against the floor, looking bored. "I've a rally to plan."

Frank tugged open his right-hand drawer to scrounge for aspirin.

"Sheriff, did you hear me?"

"Yes, loud and clear," he said, still buried in his desk. He waved at them. "Go, ladies, please, go. But if you think of anything else, give me a call."

"Good day then," Ida said briskly and rose with a clack of booted heels. "Come along, Dot," she instructed. With a shuffle of feet and slap of the door, they were gone.

Frank fished two white pills from his drawer. He blew some fuzz from them before he put them on his tongue and forced them down, grimacing at the powdery taste. But he guessed that swallowing aspiring dry wasn't half as unpleasant as putting up with Ida and Dot the better part of the morning.

He rubbed at his brow as he glanced to the yellow tablet between his elbows. Barely half the page was filled.

Good grief.

He'd talked with a handful of townsfolk this morning, and no one had told him any more than Dot and Ida.

Someone had to have seen or heard something. This town was filled with nosy neighbors who knew more about each other than many spouses. Whoever had killed Milton Grone could not have done it without some kind of slip-up. No murder — or murderer — was perfect, not outside the movies anyway.

Frank felt somewhat uneasy being at the helm of such a case. That's why he'd left the city for River Bend all those years ago. He liked packing a gun, but he didn't like using one. Here, he mostly mediated arguments, found lost pets, and kept the juvenile delinquents from stirring up trouble beyond stealing a boat for a joyride up the river. Those things, he did well. But solving a murder?

He sighed. That was a bird of a different feather. Kind of like Ida and Dot.

"Sheriff? I'm on time, aren't I?"

He looked up to see Art Beaner standing across his desk, wiping a palm across his crown to smooth down the sparse tufts of hair.

"Well, even if I'm not, at least I'm here, right?"

Art shuffled over to the chair vacated by Ida and sat stiffly.

"I played a quick round at the club over in Jerseyville, but I turned down drinks at the 19th hole. I told 'em I had a business meeting. They would have gotten too big of a kick hearing the sheriff wanted to grill me about Grone's murder. They would have ribbed me to no end." He cocked his egg-shaped noggin, peering at Frank through his glasses. "Can we get it over with as soon as possible? Bertha's got lunch waiting at home."

Frank picked up his pencil. If he wanted direct, he'd get it. "Where were you between seven and eight o'clock last Thursday night?"

Beaner placed his palms on Frank's desk, his expression incredulous. "You know damned well where I was. Everyone in town knows where I am every Thursday night at seven." He yanked a limp handkerchief from his shorts and blew his nose. Then he stuffed the cloth back in his back pocket. "I'm the chairman of the town council. Heck, I'm more the mayor of this town than Barney Plunkett. Dear God, the man's barely mobile on a good day," he muttered. "Has a cigar with his prune juice before 'Wheel of Fortune' after dinner and then he's out like a light."

The ache behind Frank's forehead thumped, and he wished the aspirin would start kicking in. "We're discussing Milton Grone not Mayor Plunkett."

"Sorry."

The sheriff tried again. "As I recall it, you and Milt didn't get along any better than the Hatfields and McCoys. You had a running feud over community dues that he owed."

"It wasn't a feud, Frank." Beaner shook a finger at him. "Merely a loud disagreement."

Frank didn't believe a word. "The man shot at you, Art."

"Maybe so," Beaner said, settling his sunburned forearms over the alligator on his chest. "But that doesn't mean I'd go and murder him, does it?"

"It gives you a motive."

"What motive?" Art guffawed. "I had a better chance getting those back-dues paid if Grone were alive and kicking, right?"

Frank leaned forward. "I'd say you had a much better shot with Grone out of the way. You could hire Stanley Horn to work the legal system and collect all those overdue fees from his estate."

"That's not a bad idea." Beaner's brow furrowed, as if chewing on the thought.

"You're a real estate broker, Art. You've probably got your eye on Grone's house, too. Had nerve enough to chat with his widow about her putting the place up for sale. You could probably get it for a song. It'd make one nice flip, as close to the river as it is."

This time, Frank saw Beaner flinch and knew he'd struck a nerve, so he pushed harder. "I'll bet you've already been chatting with your golf buddies about it, huh? Would it be nice having one of your pals from the country club living there instead of Shotsie Grone?"

Art shrugged. "So what if I brought up the subject with Milt's widow? You can't blame me for that. Life goes on." He turned red above his collar. "But I didn't kill him. I swear."

"Oh, well, if you swear to it," Frank murmured.

"There are at least thirty people who'll attest to it! My God, Frank." Art threw up his hands. "I was right there alongside Mrs. Evans when we left the town hall. I was the one who found the shotgun, remember? I didn't even know the man was dead until then, same as everyone else."

"Maybe you were late to the meeting."

"I was not!" Beaner stiffened. "I'm always there fifteen minutes early, and I didn't leave the podium until that loony-tune Ida led that lynch mob toward the Grones' place."

"Did you notice anything odd about that particular meeting?" Frank asked, taking a different tack this time, wishing now he'd gone to the meeting himself, rather than staying at home watching hockey with Sarah. Usually, the meetings bored him to tears what with all that discussion of sewage pumps and recycling projects. Though this one, it seemed, would've been worth missing a Blues shoot-out win against the Blackhawks.

Art tapped a finger to his recessed chin. "Here's how it went. Clara Foley read the minutes, as she always does. Then Ida started her song and dance about the land being sold to Wet and Woolly, and Shotsie Grone started asking questions about how much money Milton got for the deal."

"Whoa." Biddle stopped taking notes. "Shotsie Grone was there? That's not usual, is it?"

"No," Art told him and sniffed. "If you came every now and again yourself, you'd know that she's never attended even once before that night. But she made herself the center of attention, all right. Stood up in the back and asked some very direct questions about the property upriver, like what it was worth and why River Bend didn't buy it from Milton."

Frank was stunned. "She didn't know?"

"I guess Milton figured her ignorance is his bliss. Although I'm not sure as how Milt could've kept her in the dark since the newspaper's been full of stories about the deal for months."

"Maybe Shotsie doesn't read much," Frank said. Mrs. Grone was full of piss and vinegar, but he wouldn't classify her as bright. She was more like a low-watt incandescent than a crisp LED. "What happened after Shotsie spoke up?"

Beaner shrugged. "First, Shotsie and Ida started arguing and then Ida struck up the mutiny and town hall emptied out. I tried to make everyone come back, but no one paid much attention."

Biddle figured that happened to Art fairly often.

"I was one of the last to leave. Helen Evans and Dr. Fister can vouch for me. I tagged along with them. And if you can't trust a grandmother and a minister" — Beaner waggled a finger at him — "then you can't believe anyone, can you?"

"I guess not." Biddle sighed.

Art picked at invisible lint on his plaid shorts. "Are you done with me now, Sheriff? Bertha made pot roast in the crock pot for lunch, and it's the one thing she cooks that doesn't taste like shoe leather. I'd hate for her to start eating without me."

Seeing as how Bertha Beaner weighed at least twice what Art did, Frank could understand the man's fear about being late for a meal.

He set down his pen and nodded. "Go right along. I'll let you know if I need you again."

"Anytime, Frank," Beaner chirped; but, from the speed with which he hopped up from the chair and was gone, Frank had doubts that he meant it.

The sheriff scratched the stubble on his jaw and pondered what he'd just heard.

Art Beaner might be a pompous jerk, but he wasn't sure the fellow had it in him to kill. No, Beaner was too concerned with what people thought of him. Murdering Milton wouldn't be good for his image at the Jerseyville Country Club.

Frank pushed away from his desk, setting aside the yellow pad, the topmost page now filled with his chicken scratches.

A few names remained on his interview list. He'd hoped to get to them today.

But at the moment, his stomach growled. Art's mention of pot roast had him feeling mighty hungry. Surely the investigation could wait until he'd had his lunch.

He went to the door and pulled it wide, only to come face to face with Earnest Fister.

The minister looked grim, not that Frank had seen him smile any too often. Still, he always had a kind word or warm greeting.

Now, he was oddly silent.

"Pastor," Frank said, standing awkwardly there in the jamb. "Is there something I can do for you? I was on my way out . . ."

"I've a confession of sorts."

Frank grinned. "Isn't that your department not mine?"

But Fister's frown remained. "Can we do this inside, Sheriff? I'd rather keep it private."

"Of course," Frank said reluctantly, trying hard to ignore the thunderous protest of his stomach. "Come on in," he instructed and gestured for Fister to enter.

"It's about my daughter," the pastor began even before Biddle had settled back into his chair. "She was having an affair with Milton Grone."

CHAPTER TWENTY-FIVE

Helen emerged from the grocery store with her recyclable bag filled to the brim. She'd picked up all the bare necessities which, in her case, meant two dozen cans of cat food, plus a bag of dry cat food, skim milk, bananas, and bread. She paused at the curb as a car went past, then she crossed the street to the one-pump gas station.

She inquired f the owner, Dexter Bigby, was about as he'd suggested last week that she bring her Chevy in for a tune-up.

She didn't spot Dex, but she did see a familiar lime green VW bug. A moment later, a voluptuous redhead exited the tiny station, her hands fumbling inside her enormous pocketbook.

"Mrs. Grone?" Helen called out, shifting the bag in her arms so that she could wiggle her fingers. "Yoo-hoo, Delilah!"

The woman hesitated beside the VW, squinting as she drew a cigarette to her lips. "That you, Mrs. Evans?" she shouted and clomped across the concrete toward Helen in her high-heeled pumps. "Well, hey there," she said and plucked the unlit cigarette from between her lips. "The last time I saw you, the Black Widow chased me out of Milt's funeral service. Just days ago, though it feels like a week." She fiddled with her cigarette, her eyes staring down at it with obvious longing. She glanced up at Helen. "You mind if I smoke?"

Actually, Helen did, but she didn't want to run Delilah off. So, she told her, "Go right ahead."

Delilah lit up, inhaling several times deeply, before breathing the smoke out through her nose.

Funny, Helen thought, how awful the smoke smelled to her now when she herself had puffed up a storm all through college, until she'd married Joe and got pregnant.

She tried hard not to cough. "What brings you to town so soon again?"

"I, uh, ran out of gas, would you believe." Delilah jerked her chin toward the car still parked by the lone pump. "I met a friend at a winery in Grafton, then I got on the River Road head back to Alton. Only, I realized the tank was near-empty." She puffed again then shook her head. "No, that's not true. I wasn't in Grafton." She sucked on her bottom lip. "Guess it can't hurt to tell you the reason I'm back in River Bend is to see about Milt's will. I thought I'd better find out if he left it all to that bimbo of his or if he put aside a few dollars for the kids. It wouldn't make up for all those years he ignored them, of course, but it couldn't hurt a bit."

"Did you talk to his lawyer?" Helen asked, peering over the top of her grocery sack. "What did you learn?"

Delilah sucked on her cig and then blew out a stream of smoke. "What I learned from that bow-tied bozo of Milt's is that he thinks he's Perry Mason." She rolled her eyes. "Stanley Horn," she grumbled, "might be a small-town attorney but he can spout legal mumbo-jumbo with the best of 'em. When he opens his mouth and starts talking, I feel like I'm from another planet."

Helen liked Stanley Horn. The fellow was always on the up and up. He'd handled Joe's will and the family trusts, and Helen knew he was a stickler for attorney-client privilege. If Delilah and her kids weren't in Milt's will, Stanley wouldn't talk to her about it.

"Was he helpful?" Helen asked.

Delilah snorted. "All he said was I wasn't in it. I wasn't related to Milt by blood or marriage so I don't have the right to know what's in it. Blah blah blah."

Helen shifted the bag to her right hip. "Will the children inherit?"

"If they're in the will, Mr. Stanley Horn, Esquire, didn't breathe a word. He told me that we'd be notified about the reading if there was cause to do that. Then he pushed me out the door," she said, frowning, "which is no way to treat a dead man's wife."

"You're his ex-wife," Helen gently reminded.

"Like that blond ditz would ever let me forget." Delilah took a long drag off the cigarette, exhaled a gray cloud, and dropped what remained, grinding it under her heel.

Helen winced. She was tempted to quip, "The world is not your ashtray," but bit her tongue. She didn't want to tick off Delilah and scare her away while she was still yakking.

"I can't believe that piece of trash is gonna end up with all that bread," she moaned and pushed at her hairdo with crimson-tipped fingers. "What good was she to him? She didn't even give him one baby much less two. It hardly seems fair that I should get left out in the cold when I'm the one stuck raising his sons."

"On the bright side," Helen remarked as if there was one, "I think it might be a while before the court divides up Milton's estate."

"Oh?" Delilah's gaze locked on Helen. "And why's that?"

"What with his being murdered," Helen started but stopped when she heard Delilah's quick intake of breath. "You hadn't heard?"

"I did . . . I did! But I still can't believe it," Delilah sputtered. She had her hand on her heart as if about to spout the Pledge of Allegiance. "It still doesn't seem real, even though I read that piece in this morning's *Telegraph*."

"It was a shock to us all."

"It's freaking nuts," Delilah said. "He was hit in the head, is that right? The paper said the weapon was a shovel that belonged to that stuck-up English lady next door."

"Um-hmm," Helen made a noncommittal noise. She did not want to drag poor Felicity into the conversation.

"Does the sheriff know who did it?" Delilah cocked her head.

Helen shifted the grocery sack to her left hip. "He's investigating."

"No arrests?"

"Not yet."

"It might take awhile." Delilah laughed. "With all the people that hated Milton around here, I figure the sheriff has a suspect list a mile long."

"Since we're on the subject," Helen said and glanced up Main Street, "perhaps you should stop by the station and talk to Frank Biddle yourself."

"Me?" Her penciled eyebrows arched.

"Well, you did say you came in town on Thursday night to see your ex-husband," Helen said, reminding Delilah of her remarks after the funeral. "You told me you found him there on the ground when you arrived."

"What are you saying, Mrs. Evans?" She plunged her hand inside her purse, no doubt in search of another cigarette. "You're not implying that I had anything to do with his untimely death?"

The grocery sack felt suddenly heavy. "I'm not implying anything," Helen assured her. "But you might know more than you think."

"Maybe you're right." Delilah pulled a compact from her bag and popped it open. She checked her face in the tiny mirror, then began rubbing lipstick from her teeth. "The killer could have still been hanging around when I was there." She snapped her compact shut and shuddered. "It gives me the creeps to think about it."

Helen dared to ask, "Why didn't you call for help when you found him?"

Delilah's face tightened. "Like I told you before, Mrs. Evans, I heard all those voices coming up toward the house, and I didn't want to be standing there kneeling over him. I know running off wasn't the smartest thing to do but I was scared. Besides, what good could my asking for help have done? Even Doc Melville couldn't have revived a dead man."

That much was true, Helen thought. "No one saw you that night?"

"I don't think so. Milt didn't even realize I was driving in after my shift. Every time I called, he hung up on me, remember?" Delilah's eyes welled suddenly. "I just wanted what was rightfully mine."

Helen nodded, feeling sorry for Delilah and women like her who had marriages that failed and, even worse, husbands who abandoned their children.

Delilah sucked in a deep breath. "You figure I should talk to the sheriff?"

"I do," Helen said. "Just tell him exactly what you told me. That you arrived in River Bend before eight."

"I couldn't get here any sooner," Delilah told her, "I had to change my clothes first. I didn't want to have to face old Milt in my pink polyester number with grease and coffee splattered all over my apron."

So, Delilah had likely arrived just before the mob from town hall marched up the street toward the Grones' house. Helen wondered if perhaps the killer had still been around when Delilah saw Milt on the ground.

Before Helen knew it, Delilah was shaking another cigarette out of the pack. She involuntarily made a face, and Delilah picked up on it.

"I know," Milton's ex-wife said. "It's a nasty habit."

And expensive, Helen silently added.

"I was tryin' to quit but this whole business has shot my nerves to hell." She shrugged and pulled out her lighter.

Certain that she'd inhaled her quota of second-hand smoke for one afternoon, Helen hugged her bag to her chest, feeling as if the sack had doubled its weight in the past ten minutes. She told Delilah, "I should get home. Amber will shred the place if I don't fix him some lunch soon."

The redhead squinted. "Amber?"

"My cat."

"Ah." The cigarette bouncing on her lips, Delilah commented, "I like pets well enough," she said. "It was Milton who despised 'em."

"I heard," Helen said, hardly able to remember the number of times she'd listened to Felicity complaining about Grone taking pot-shots at poor Kitty.

"Well, it was nice seeing you again, Mrs. Evans," Delilah said, waving her cigarette as she walked to her car.

Helen headed up the sidewalk and had gotten but a few yards ahead, when several riotous bangs stopped her dead in her tracks.

For heaven's sake!

She turned see the green VW noisily pulling out of the gas station, rattling and rumbling as it chugged onto Main Street.

Helen watched the car go and frowned. She would bet all two dozen cans of cat food in her sack that it wasn't the last the town would see of Delilah Grone, at least not until things were settled with Milt's estate. And if Delilah didn't get what she wanted? Helen didn't doubt that the first Mrs. Grone would fight the second Mrs. Grone tooth and nail for every penny, kind of like Godzilla vs. Mothra on the late-late movie.

Helen shook her head and continued toward home.

CHAPTER TWENTY-SIX

Once Amber had devoured his can of Catch o' the Day and Helen had gobbled down some chicken salad, she settled down on the porch and propped her bifocals on her nose. She picked up her purple pen and Sunday's edition of the *Telegraph,* folded to expose the crossword puzzle. Its squares were only half-filled as she hadn't had the chance to finish without interruption since she'd started in on it the day before.

Four down: a three-letter word for male swan.

She scrunched her brow, tapping the pen against her chin until a slow smile curved upon her mouth.

She put the purple tip to the squares and scratched out "cob."

Five down: a nine-letter word for Alexander Graham Bell's invention.

The telephone rang.

Helen slapped down her pen and slipped off her glasses.

She marched into the house from the porch to stop the intrusive chirping. A nine-letter word for Bell's invention. Phooey! That was too easy. She didn't need such an obvious hint.

She snatched up the receiver from her old-fangled wall phone. "Hello?" she said briskly.

"Helen!" The agitated voice was Felicity's. "Can you get here and fast? The sheriff's on his way up. I can see his auto on the road! I've a dreadful feeling he's coming to arrest me!"

With only a terse, "I'm on my way," Helen hung up and grabbed her keys. Not two minutes after, she screeched to a stop in front of Felicity's.

Biddle's car sat on the shoulder of the road nearer to the Grones' house.

As Helen parked and exited her Chevy, Felicity flew out through the screened door and scuttled down the steps. One hand clutched at her hat, the other at her heart.

"What's going on?" Helen asked, confused. "Where is he?"

"He wasn't coming after me," her friend answered breathlessly. She tipped her head toward her neighbor's. "He's in the yard next door, poking through the weeds."

Helen glanced past the wood fence. Sure enough, there was Frank Biddle, clad in his uniform of dusty tan, prodding an overgrown rhododendron with a stick.

"What's he looking for?" she asked.

"Something to do with the murder, I'm sure." Felicity wiped her palms down the sides of her housedress. "I can't imagine what it might be."

Helen started off across the lawn only to have Felicity call her back.

"What, in God's name, are you doing?"

"I want to see what he's up to," she answered, squinting through the afternoon sun at Felicity's worried face, watching her from beneath the cock-eyed hat brim. "Maybe I'll learn something new."

"Such as?"

"I'll let you know," Helen said over her shoulder as she continued walking, her sneakered feet squishing in the grass.

She waved as Biddle glanced up. Then she ducked between the rails of the fence rather than go around it, though it took a good deal of wiggling to get through. Before she had a chance to join Biddle and ask him a single question, the Grones' screened door slapped open and shut.

Shotsie came outside, her hands on her hips and eyes narrowed. The frown on her lips underscored her disapproval. "What exactly do you think you're doing, snooping around here like that?" she snapped at them, stomping forward. "Don't you need some kind of permit before you can traipse around my place like you own it?"

"It's called a warrant, ma'am," Biddle said.

"What?"

"A warrant, Mrs. Grone," he repeated, "not a permit. And, no, I don't need one to search a crime scene. All I need is this." He patted the star-shaped badge at his breast with a dirt smudged finger. "I'm looking for evidence."

"Will it take long?" Shotsie asked, pushing at the limp curls on her brow. "'Cause it gives me the creeps having you sneak around like a burglar. My nerves aren't too good as it is, you understand."

"I do," Biddle assured her. The sideways look he cast at Helen indicated he was anxious to get on with it himself. "Just give me an hour."

"A whole hour? What else do you expect to find?" Shotsie looked confused. "You've got the shovel that did it. All you've got to do now is put that snooty Miss Timmons in the slammer."

Helen stepped out of Biddle's shadow. "Just because the murder weapon belongs to Felicity doesn't mean she killed your husband. Anyone could have taken it from her yard and used it."

"But her fingerprints were on it, weren't they?" Shotsie remarked. "Everyone in town knows that."

Helen opened her mouth, but Biddle cleared his throat in warning. She shut her trap and let him speak.

"Yes, Miss Timmons' prints were on her shovel. They were the only prints, and there were few enough of them." He absently beat at the knee-high weeds with the stick in his hands. "It almost seems as though someone tried to wipe the handle clean."

That was the first Helen had heard of that. "Isn't that suspicious?"

Biddle nodded. "It is to me."

Shotsie scowled. "What it proves is that the nutcase killed Milt! She hit him with her old shovel then tried to ditch it in the bushes behind her house. Even I can see it as plain as the big, fat nose on your face!"

"Maybe you should go back inside," Helen said sharply, "and let the sheriff investigate."

"Oh, yeah?" Shotsie curled her hands to fists. "So now you're the Queen of River Bend, telling me what to do?"

"Someone has to."

"Ladies, please! Stop bickering." Biddle slapped the stick against his opened palm like a pot-bellied Patton. "Now if both of you would please leave me in peace. I've got things to do." He walked away, his head bent as he continued his search, nudging uprooted rocks and pushing at clusters of weeds with his stick.

Helen looked hard at Shotsie. She was finding it difficult to sympathize with her after all her efforts to blame Felicity.

Though she knew she should go as the sheriff had suggested, Helen found herself marching toward Shotsie. When she was close enough, she told her in a low voice, "I realize you're angry, my dear, but you must stop accusing Felicity of murder. You might as well point your finger at the minister."

Helen half-expected Shotsie to blow up again, shaking her tiny fists and screaming. But she didn't. Instead, Shotsie laughed.

"You're right," the blonde said and tucked her arms beneath her breasts. "I *should* point a finger at Fister. He had as much reason as anyone to want Miltie dead, considering how his slutty daughter tried to trap my husband."

Helen stood there, stunned. So, Milton Grone *was* the older, married man who'd fooled around with Maddy Fister. Helen had her suspicions, particularly after her strange conversation with Earnest Fister just that morning. But how long, she wondered, had Shotsie known?

"The wife is always the last to learn, right, Mrs. Evans?" Shotsie said. Rather than rant and rave, Shotsie seemed to deflate. She shrugged and stared at her slippers. When she finally looked up again, her face was drawn, the lines around her mouth and her eyes deeper. She seemed to have aged a decade in minutes. "It was ugly," she said softly, tugging on the cuffs of her cardigan. "Milt threw it right in my face after we'd had another fight before bed. He said he was tired of my nagging, that if I didn't like how he lived his life I should just leave like Delilah had and it'd be no skin off his back."

Helen murmured, "I'm sorry," and she was. There was so much about Milton Grone she hadn't known, so many ways he'd hurt the people around him again and again. It was a wonder he'd stayed alive as long as he had.

"He told me he had a young thing falling all over him, but he didn't say he'd knocked her up," she added, blinking back tears. "I found that nugget out on my own. People tell secrets in awful loud voices sometimes."

She'd overhead? But how, Helen mused? The day that Madeline miscarried only Fanny and Amos Melville were around besides Madeline's father, and Earnest Fister certainly wouldn't have gossiped about such a thing, nor would Doc. Helen hadn't mentioned it to a soul so that left one other person. *Damn you*, Fanny, she thought.

"Why did he do it?" Shotsie asked, as much to herself as to Helen. "I tried to sort that out, too. I thought he loved me, and maybe he did once. But this deal with Wet 'n' Woolly changed him. He started acting funny, like he was tired of me, tired of us. I guess he liked having a teenager lusting after him."

"Why didn't you—" Helen started to ask.

"Kick him out?" Shotsie finished, taking the words right out of her mouth. She shrugged. "He was my husband. He was all I had. I wasn't gonna lose him to high school senior." She jerked her chin, eyes glistening. "He never would've left me for her, no matter what he said. I think he mostly did it just to get Fister's goat."

"Oh, dear, I'm so sorry."

"Don't do that, okay?" Shotsie waved Helen away. "Don't look at me that way. Don't pity me. If you do, I'll throw up." She pulled the cuffs of her sweater down her hands and glanced up at the sky. The pale ringlets of her hair swirled across her round cheeks.

At that instance, the woman looked more a waif than a widow, and Helen almost forgave her for accusing Felicity of being a killer.

"I think I'll go in now and try to get some rest," Shotsie whispered. "I haven't gotten much sleep lately."

"I'll bet you haven't eaten much either. Would you like me to come in and fix you something?" Helen offered.

Shotsie shook her head. "I'd rather be alone, if you don't mind."

"Are you sure?"

"I'm sure." Shotsie didn't even turn at Helen's voice. She trudged up the porch steps and slipped inside.

Helen stared at the screened door for a while after, feeling a bit guilty at being so hard on Grone's widow. The poor thing had a lot more on her mind than Helen could have imagined, as if Milton's unnatural death wasn't enough.

She went over to where Frank Biddle stooped over a tangle of tall grass. "Have you found something?" she asked, putting her hands on her knees and leaning over. All she could see with her own eyes was a few rusted beer cans, some candy wrappers, and cigarette butts.

He flipped whatever it was into his palm and smiled a Cheshire cat grin. "A brass casing," he said. "It's probably from Grone's shotgun, the one Art Beaner found in the bushes."

"Just one shell?" Helen asked.

"Only one."

Helen followed behind him as he picked his way across the yard to a bald spot of dirt between patches of crabgrass. In its center was a craggy rock, its rough surface splotched with rusty-brown. It was the stone Milton's head had been resting on, she realized, and felt her stomach lurch.

"Here's what I figure," Biddle said, gesticulating as he spoke. "Grone came out of the house with his shotgun loaded. Maybe he heard a noise like Miss Timmons' cat prowling around. The perp took him by surprise, smacking him in the head with the shovel. The shotgun goes off when it hits the ground." He flipped over the brass casing in his hand. "I'll wager the shot went straight in the air."

Helen followed his gaze up to where the trees arched above. She hoped the bullet hadn't hit an unsuspecting bird in its nest.

Biddle slipped the shell into his pocket. "I don't imagine Grone even saw it coming. If he had . . . well, he had the shotgun ready, didn't he? He could've picked off someone lunging at him with a shovel and blown a hole in 'em as big as my fist."

"So?" Helen wasn't sure what it all meant.

He met her gaze, head-on. "So, unless there's someone walking around town with a hole in his gut, then the killer's still alive and well and lying low in River Bend, hoping he flies under my radar."

Unless it wasn't a he, but a *she*, Helen mused.

CHAPTER TWENTY-SEVEN

Frank Biddle picked up the telephone and dialed, tapping his pen against the papers on his desk while he waited for the ringing to start.

He re-read a note left by Delilah Grone. She'd apparently come by his office when he'd been out to lunch. "Mrs. Evans told me to get in touch," said the loopy cursive, "I was in River Bend the night Milt was killed." She'd left a phone number scrawled at the bottom of the page.

"Roadside Rest Stop," a weary voice answered after half a dozen rings. Frank could hear the noise of chatter and the clatter of dishes in the background. When he asked for Delilah, he was informed in an impatient shout, "Delilah don't come in on Mondays. Try again tomorrow afternoon."

The line clicked in his ear.

He stared at the receiver in his hand, wondering why the first Mrs. Grone hadn't left her cell or home phone number. He turned the note over, hoping to find a second number on the back; but it was blank. If Delilah was in River Bend last Thursday night, Frank figured he'd check a few facts in the meantime. So, he punched in her work number again.

It took a full dozen rings this time before anyone picked up.

When he asked for the manager, he initially got resistance. But when he said, "Would your boss rather the Sheriff of River Bend, Illinois, show up at the Roadside Rest Stop in full uniform with the bubble-light rolling on the squad car?" he quickly got action. Soon enough, a gruff voice that claimed to be in charge asked, "What can I do you for, Officer? But whatever it is, can you make it snappy? Time's short, and so am I."

Frank asked if Delilah Grone had been at work last Thursday evening. The manager put him on hold to look up the schedule; "on hold" in this case meaning the phone was apparently dropped with a clatter and Biddle found himself listening to the cacophony of the rest-stop restaurant until the growler got back on the line.

"Sheriff, you still there?"

"I'm here!" Biddle felt like he had to shout so the fellow could hear his reply above the racket.

"Delilah's shift was from eleven to seven that night and, as far as I know, she didn't skip out. If she did and I'd heard about it, she'd be standing in the unemployment line right about now."

As far as he knew, Biddle thought, not liking that phrase in the least. "Weren't you around to keep an eye on the place?"

"Not that day," the manager replied. "I had one of those twenty-four-hour bugs that kept me on the john half the day."

Biddle didn't want him to expound so he followed up quickly with, "Can I talk to anyone else who was on the same shift, someone who could verify whether Delilah stayed and worked until seven?"

The man grumbled, not sounding thrilled at giving out the information. "Velma Simms," he said brusquely. "You can catch her here tomorrow in the a.m. if you want. She's off today, too."

Biddle was about to thank the man for his trouble but the line clicked off.

He hung up and began to scratch a few notes on his legal pad regarding Delilah Grone, in particular that she worked until seven on the night Milton died. Frank had looked up the address of the truck stop which was twenty miles due south of Alton. If Delilah had driven to River Bend straight from there, it would have taken her a good forty-five minutes to an hour. If she'd stopped anywhere in between, she wouldn't have made it to River Bend until Milt was already dead.

A few minutes here and there made a pretty big difference, he knew, and he decided to go see Velma Sims at the rest-stop restaurant personally the next morning. It was too easy for people to lie on the phone. Frank wanted to see her eyes. The eyes always told the truth.

He shuffled papers until he found the list he'd made with suspects to interview. It had two names freshly added: Earnest Fister and his daughter Madeline.

He put aside the pen and rubbed his eyes.

Instead of his list getting smaller, the number of suspects only seemed to have grown. The deeper he poked into Milton Grone's murder, the more motives he dug up. Although most all of those under suspicion appeared to have an alibi for the time of the crime, Frank didn't believe everything was so clear-cut. Folks didn't always remember things straight. The brain was a tricky organ. Sometimes it got mixed up.

River Bend was a community of two hundred people. To call it small was an understatement. It was only a mile from one end of town to the other, which would have made it pretty simple for someone to show up at the town meeting on Thursday, duck out then return fifteen minutes later with no one the wiser.

He thumbed through his notes from the interviews thus far, trying to pick out any discrepancies. Though he stared and stared, he could find no blatant holes, nothing that reached out and grabbed him.

Ida Bell and Dot Feeny were at town hall, something board chairman Art Beaner verified, which afforded him an alibi of his own. Felicity Timmons had been there, too, right beside Helen Evans. Earnest Fister had conveniently been on Mrs. Evans' other side.

Madeline Fister claimed to have been home all evening, watching TV in the house she shared with her father, just a block from the Grones'. She said she fell asleep on the couch and was awakened by the toll of the chapel bell, which would have rung at eight o'clock when the town meeting ended. She did admit to hearing some loud pops, like the fireworks on July Fourth, sometime before then. But they could've come from the television, she'd told him, as she'd had a cop show on when she'd dropped off.

What if those pops weren't from the TV? Maybe the noise from the show had disguised Milt's shotgun going off. That would have fit in Biddle's timeline for the murder but it didn't help Maddy. Her alibi was hardly airtight.

Frank drew a question mark beside the girl's name.

* * *

The sheriff had interviewed Fister's daughter only after the preacher had dragged the girl in by the arm and ordered her to talk. She'd tried to act tough, but Frank saw that she was afraid. And she had good reason. Fister had informed him about Grone's affair with the girl and how Grone had gotten her pregnant before he'd dumped her. Could she have struck Milton with the shovel after he'd broken her heart?

Or had the pastor done the deed himself, so angry at the older man for taking advantage of his daughter that he'd forgotten all about the Commandment that said, "Thou shall not kill?"

Frank drew a question mark beside the minister's name as well.

The weight of the case hung around him like an albatross. He frowned and closed up the file, shoving it into his top drawer. Then he rose from his chair and stretched his back, eliciting an unsettling series of pops.

He plunked on his hat and closed up shop, heading home to Sarah and dinner of tuna casserole; though the questions about Milton's murder wouldn't leave his head. They flooded his every thought, turning them as thick and muddy as the Mississippi River.

CHAPTER TWENTY-EIGHT

Helen had intended to cancel her Monday night bridge party because of Milton Grone's murder and its aftermath. But when she'd called around, her plan had met with such resistance that she'd decided the show would go on.

"Why on earth would we miss bridge?" Clara Foley had gasped. "To honor the memory of Milton Grone? Please!"

The sentiment had been echoed, more or less, by all the girls.

Helen pushed her wicker to the walls and set up three card tables with folding chairs on the porch. By seven o'clock, the rise and fall of laughter and voices filled the air like summer cicadas.

Helen sat between Fanny Melville and Bebe Horn, attorney Stanley's wife. Her partner, Clara Foley, glanced at the hand she'd been dealt and then up at Helen. Her plump face broke out in a grin. "We're hot today," she declared, "hotter than a witch's . . ."

"Clara," Helen sent her a look of warning, "no table-talk."

Fanny Melville peered through her bifocals at the score pad near Helen's right elbow. "Well, I hope you can open," she said to Bebe. "The way we're playing, I don't think even one of Doc's Vitamin-B shots could revive our score."

"Yeah, that's the spirit," Bebe said and shook her head. She gave her hand a final once-over before she announced, "I bid one no-trump."

"What an optimist you are!" Clara chuckled. "The only way you'll pull this off is if Fanny has some cards up her sleeve."

"Oh, hush up, would you, and let's get on with the game," Helen said, wishing she'd partnered with Lola Mueller or Bertha Beaner, anyone who didn't talk so much. She was in no mood for chatter. No mood for bridge, to be honest.

She had too much on her mind, though the aftermath of Milton's murder didn't seem to be troubling the others in her bridge group. She sighed impatiently then prodded Clara. "Go on and bid, please. We haven't got forever."

"Okay, okay." Clara checked her hand. "Guess I'll double that no trump of yours, Bebe," she declared, looking smug.

"Fanny," Helen said, trying to nudge the game along. If the pace didn't pick up, it was certainly going to be a long evening. "Hurry up."

Fanny rearranged several cards fanned out in her hands with a frown. She looked up at Bebe and shrugged. "Sorry, hon, but it looks like I'm gonna have to pass."

Helen smiled. Perhaps this game wouldn't drag on forever after all. "Two hearts," she said to Fanny's moan and Bebe's grimace.

"Good goin', partner," Clara cheered and slapped the tabletop.

"If I didn't know better," Fanny muttered, "I'd say the deck was stacked."

As Bebe had dealt this round, she glanced over at Fanny, looking apologetic. Then she stared at her cards for a full minute before murmuring, "Oh, my. I'll have to pass as well."

"C'mon, Bebe," Clara teased, "where's your killer instinct? I mean, you are married to a shark. Some of it should've rubbed off after all these years."

Helen chuckled.

But Bebe seemed not to take offense. "Like I haven't heard every lawyer joke there is," she said with a laugh.

"Speaking of Stanley—" Bebe leaned over the table. "Guess who showed up at his office this morning?" Before anyone could say a word in response, she announced, "Mrs. Grone!"

Though it was no surprise to Helen, Clara and Fanny seemed to eat it up.

"Shotsie?" Fanny inquired.

"No, no," Bebe replied and toyed with her cards. "Not the current wife, the first one, Delilah. She wanted to know about Milton's will."

"Well, butter my biscuits," Clara quipped, her eyes wide. "I didn't think she'd show her face in this town again after what happened at the church during Milton's funeral."

"Do tell," Fanny said, egging her on. "Is she getting anything? Judging by how much they fought before their divorce, I can't believe he'd leave her a penny."

Bebe shifted in her seat, looking around her before she said in a whisper, "I'm not supposed to gossip about Stanley's clients."

Clara snorted. "It's not like you haven't done it before."

Even Fanny clicked tongue against teeth. "You know it won't go past us."

Helen had to press her mouth shut or she'd have snapped at Fanny about talking out of turn about Madeline Fister. Now wasn't that time. She'd deal with Fanny later.

"All right, all right, since you insist," Bebe said, giving in, her voice barely audible as she confessed, "Delilah isn't mentioned in the will at all and neither are her kids."

Clara shrugged. "That doesn't surprise me in the least. Milton Grone never cared about anyone but himself."

Fanny lifted her eyebrows. "If that's true then Delilah had no motive to kill him, did she?"

"Was she a suspect?" Bebe asked.

"Who isn't?" Clara remarked.

"Girls, please," Helen chastised. "Let's get back to the cards."

But no one seemed to listen.

"If the sheriff suspected Delilah it was probably because she was the only one of Milton's enemies who wasn't at the town meeting on Thursday," Clara said. "You were there, weren't you, Bebe?"

"Yes, but we snuck in late. Stan had to meet with a client in Grafton and I went along, so we missed the first few minutes."

Helen hadn't recalled seeing them at all. But the hall had been unusually full so it was impossible to remember all the faces.

"Were you in the back?" she asked. "Somewhere near Shotsie Grone?"

Bebe pressed a finger to her chin. "I do remember looking around when the ruckus started, and there she was. But I hadn't noticed her before."

"She made a point to be seen," Clara drawled. "Talk about stealing the show! I'm surprised Art Beaner didn't have a stroke, losing control the way he did. And then Ida nearly took a swing at Shotsie before she stormed out like General MacArthur."

"Ahem." Helen cleared her throat. "Girls, do you imagine we could get back to the game? Or is it going to be called on account of gossip?"

Clara didn't look pleased but did pick up her hand.

Fanny and Bebe exchanged glances then the latter meekly asked, "Does anyone know whose turn it was?"

Within an hour, they'd played out the cards, and Helen and Clara had emerged victorious again.

Helen slipped away to the kitchen as the other two tables finished their games. She retrieved a pitcher of tea from the refrigerator and was pouring it when Fanny walked in.

"What's going on with you, Helen? You're being a real party pooper tonight," Doc's wife remarked as she plucked a glass of tea from the tray. "And don't tell me it has to do with Grone's death. You didn't like the man any better than the rest of us."

"No, I didn't," Helen murmured and finished filling all the glasses.

"So why are you so gloomy? I've never known you to pooh-pooh us enjoying a good chat during bridge before."

Helen set aside the pitcher and turned to face her friend. "Since you asked," she said and crossed her arms, glaring at the familiar bespectacled face. "I'm a little bit angry with you."

"With me?" Fanny's jaw dropped. "Whatever for?"

"You flapped your gums about Madeline Fister."

"I did what?"

"You promised to keep what happened in Doc's office a secret but you must've gone and shot your mouth off . . ."

"I did no such thing!" Fanny interrupted, turning red from her lace collar to her hairline. "If someone blabbed, it wasn't me."

"Well, it certainly wasn't Earnest Fister or Amos," Helen said, standing her ground. "And I know I didn't do it, which only leaves you."

Fanny sniffed, clearly offended. "You're wrong, I tell you. It wasn't me."

"Then how in the world did Shotsie Grone find out that Maddy was pregnant?"

"Shotsie Grone knew? Why would she even care — oh, my." Fanny stared, such a shocked look on her face that Helen realized Fanny hadn't known about Madeline's affair with Milton. "Are you saying it was Milton who . . . that Maddy's baby was . . . that they were . . . ?"

"Eeeek!"

A scream reverberated through the house, and Fanny's question was lost.

"My God, it's a bunny!" a second yell followed, "and it's hanging from the cat's mouth!"

Oh, Amber, Helen thought and sidestepped Fanny. She pulled on a pair of oven mitts with the efficiency of a surgeon. Then she marched out to the porch, finding her guests teetering atop the furniture and squealing like little girls.

"Do something, Helen!" Clara Foley demanded from her perch atop the wicker settee.

She spotted Amber beneath a card table, sitting proudly on his haunches. A very small rabbit dangled from his jaws. If Helen hadn't known better, she'd have sworn the old tom was grinning at the fuss.

"You do know how to make an entrance," she said and squatted down, her mitted hands outstretched.

The cat leapt away, eluding her grasp. He dashed under the chairs that held her guests, eliciting another round of shrieks.

Helen pursued the killer feline, finally cornering him in the bathroom and prying the would-be prey from his mouth.

"No cause for alarm," she told the girls as she walked past them, the bunny cradled in her mitts. "It's not dead, merely stunned," she explained to their chorus of groans.

She headed out the screened door and deposited the trembling creature in the bushes across the road. Helen waited until it had wiggled deep into the shrubs. Then she whispered, "You're one lucky rabbit, a lot luckier than Milton Grone."

CHAPTER TWENTY-NINE

"Sheriff Biddle!"

Frank heard the voice through his opened window and slowed the patrol car to a stop alongside the stretch of blooming flowers better known as Serenity Garden.

It was half past seven on Tuesday morning. Frank had figured that, if he drove down early to the truck stop to talk to Velma Simms, he'd be back at his office well before noon. Plus, he could get himself a breakfast of sausage and eggs while he was there without Sarah leaning over his shoulder, henpecking about his cholesterol.

"Good morning, Sheriff."

"Morning, ma'am," he said, tipping his hat as Helen Evans approached the window. "You up and walking this early?" he asked, noting her blue sweatsuit and sneakers.

"Best time to do it." She drew in a deep breath. "The air smells freshest right after dawn."

"Really?" Frank took in a big gulp of the stuff himself, scrunching up his face as he caught a whiff of fish and muck from off the river. He coughed to clear the taste from his mouth, a part of him understanding then why Ida Bell was so militant about the environment hereabouts.

"You going somewhere?" she inquired.

"I am," he said and tapped his fingers on the steering wheel, eager to be off, but hardly anxious to confide his destination. He knew Helen well enough to realize she'd probably invite herself along, and Biddle didn't need a nosy grandmother — as nice as she was — playing his sidekick when he questioned Velma Simms. "I'm, uh, just heading to the station," he told her and smiled.

"You are not," she insisted, frowning at him like a disapproving schoolmarm. "You're driving in the opposite direction. Why, you're nearly to the highway already!"

"All right, you got me." He pushed up his cap and scratched his head.

He'd bet she'd been the kind of mother who, from two floors up, could hear the cookie jar lid being removed ever so gently; the kind who, years later, could recall who'd sent her thank you notes after every Christmas; and who could easily read a lie on someone's face.

"As a matter of fact," he said, giving in, "I'm on my way to a truck stop south of Alton. I need to talk to a waitress who worked the shift last Thursday night with Delilah Grone."

"You spoke to Delilah?"

"Not yet, but I did get her note," he said. "I already talked to her manager, and I want to get my timeline straight before she comes in."

"Delilah told me she arrived in River Bend just before eight and found her ex-husband dead," Helen mentioned, seeming to know as much as Frank, if not more. "If she was being honest and didn't leave work until seven, then took the time to change out of her uniform, she couldn't have been in town long before the group of us from town hall saw him lying on the ground."

Frank was tempted to say, "Oh, yeah? You know so much, maybe you should run for sheriff next term!" But, instead, he bit the inside of his cheek. "So, you and the first Mrs. Grone have gotten cozy?"

Helen looked at him strangely. "Hardly that. I did chat with her on Saturday morning after the funeral and then I bumped into her yesterday. I encouraged her to see you."

"Yes, that's what her note said, and I appreciate it, ma'am." Frank cleared his throat. "Now if you'll excuse me," he said, glancing at his wristwatch.

"Oh, yes, you were leaving for the truck stop."

"I need to talk with—"

"The waitress who shares Delilah's shifts," Helen repeated what he'd told her a moment before, a smile on her lips, one that made Frank nervous.

Surely, she hadn't already had a "chat" with Velma Simms? If Helen Evans was that good at sniffing out information, she really *should* run for sheriff. "You haven't met up with Ms. Simms, have you, Mrs. Evans?" he asked.

"No, I haven't," she said. "But I should." She drew away from the window and walked around the hood, ending up on the passenger's side of the squad car. The handle clicked, and she had the door open so quickly that Biddle could only stare as she slid in beside him and buckled up.

What the heck was she doing?

"I'm on official business, Mrs. Evans," he croaked.

"Don't worry. I have no intention of interfering," she assured him, laying her hands demurely in her lap. "But I could use a cup of coffee, and I'll bet the truck stop makes it good and strong."

Frank wanted to order her out of the car. He wanted to be angry with her for butting in, but he couldn't. Instead, he chuckled. "Do you read Agatha Christie, ma'am?"

"Now and again," she said.

"Well, I'm beginning to think you've got a Miss Marple complex. You know, the old lady snoop—"

"Yes, I know good and well." She arched her thick, gray eyebrows, but he could see the twinkle in her eyes. Then she busied herself rolling down the window enough to allow the breeze in. "Some around here might call me a busybody," she said, "but I'm just a people-person with a curious soul."

Frank didn't touch that one. He figured it might get him into trouble to speak his mind. If his twenty-year marriage to Sarah had taught him one thing it was this: the key to getting along well with women was in knowing when to shut the heck up.

Without another word, he took his foot off the brake and hit the gas, guiding the car out of town and onto the River Road.

* * *

Twenty minutes later, they entered Alton's city limits and that was with Biddle driving no faster than sixty (Helen had kept an eye on the speedometer). It took at least twenty minutes more before Helen saw the checkerboard sign for the truck stop looming over the interstate.

The sheriff pulled into a lot filled with big rigs, garnering stares from several patrons exiting the restaurant. As she got out of the car, Helen could see a good-sized crowd beyond the plate-glass windows.

"Looks like it's a popular place," she said.

Frank Biddle hurried ahead and grabbed open the door before Helen could lift a hand. As soon as she entered, her nose filled with the welcoming odors of frying bacon and coffee. At least ten pots merrily percolated atop a line of burners beneath a stainless-steel shelf that opened into the kitchen.

She followed Biddle up to the counter, where a dozen men in plaid shirts perched atop red vinyl stools. A few had their eyes glued to their phones or to newspapers. The rest bent over steaming plates of food, greedily shoveling in hash browns and pancakes.

Biddle waved a hand in the air, trying to catch the attention of the waitress who buzzed back and forth behind the length of Formica. She breezed past them once, uttering cheerily, "Be with you in a minute!" Before she took off again.

In the meanwhile, Helen perused a plastic-coated menu.

"Sorry to keep you folks waiting," the waitress said, reappearing in a bustle of pink polyester, her netted brown hair pulled away from her face. In a blink, she had her order pad out of her apron and poised in her hand, pencil at the ready. "What'll it be?"

"Coffee, please. Decaf, if you have it," Helen said.

"We sure do." The waitress grabbed a fresh pot and filled Helen's cup in a blink. "What about you, Sheriff?" she asked, eyeing his badge. "You want a shot of joe, too? Caffeinated, I'll bet."

"Actually, I'm looking for Velma Simms," he said, tugging off his hat. "I'm Sheriff Frank Biddle from River Bend. I phoned yesterday and spoke with the boss."

"Ah, I see." She put away the coffee pot and wedged the pencil above her ear. "Hank said a cop called asking some questions about Delilah's shift last Thursday. So does it have to do with her ex-husband's murder?"

Biddle flushed. "Yes, ma'am."

"Are you Miss Simms, by chance?" Helen asked, peeling off the foil skin from a thimble of cream and adding it to her coffee.

"In the flesh," she said, only to be drowned out by the ding of a bell from the kitchen.

"Velma! Pick up!" someone yelled, and, with a shrug, she slipped away only to scurry past with her skinny arms agilely balancing six steaming plates.

Helen followed her pink form as she unloaded at one table, then scurried over to an empty booth to pick up a tip and wipe the cluttered surface clean. She took an order here, another there until, again, the bell dinged again madly.

Helen felt tired just watching.

Biddle got himself a doughnut from a nearby cake-stand and devoured it in record time. He was just licking off the sugary tips of his fingers when Velma reemerged behind the counter.

"You want Velma? You've got her!" she said, tucking a food-spotted towel into the waist of her apron. She wasn't even breathing hard, Helen noticed with admiration, thinking that there was much that motherhood and waitressing had in common. Only mothers never got tips. "Is Delilah in trouble?"

"Not yet," Biddle replied, wiping his hands on a napkin. "I just need to check on her whereabouts last Thursday night. She worked the eleven-to-seven shift with you, right?"

"Uh-huh," Velma said, sticking her elbows on the counter and leaning over them. "Just like every Thursday."

Biddle nodded. He took a spiral notebook from his pocket and flipped it open to a clean sheet. He touched the tip of the tiny pencil to his tongue, before asking, "So Delilah didn't take off early?"

"No, sir," Velma said almost too quickly then she bit her lip. "At least, I don't think so but one shift starts to blur into the next."

Her eyes drifted up toward the ceiling, and Helen found herself looking up as well. All she saw were several cracks in the plaster and what looked like a grease stain or three.

"No, wait a sec, I take that back," Velma remarked with a snap of her fingers. "She did scoot a bit early. She told me there was something she had to do. That it was important. I told her I'd cover for her. No problem." She leaned in closer. "Hank was out that day with the runs so I figured what the hell? Things were pretty slow."

Biddle scribbled in his book.

Helen took a sip of her coffee then asked Velma, "Are you and Delilah close?"

"We like each other well enough," the waitress said, bobbing her head. "Not that we have much time to chew the fat because this place gets crazy-busy. But when the old dogs are barking, we take a break outside and share a cigarette."

"You know Delilah's history?" Helen went on.

Velma tipped her head. "Like where she's from?"

"More like, about her family," Helen said.

The woman's eyes brightened. "Yeah, sure, Delilah tells me about her kids, how they're doing at school." She leaned in with a wink. "All the scrapes they get into. She says the boys are like their daddy, always in trouble with the ladies." She shook her head. "I told her she had to put her foot down, but I don't think she ever listened to me. I have a couple of young'uns myself, and if you don't keep a close eye on them these days with all that sexting and bullying . . ."

Ding went the bell.

"Velma! Pick up!"

The waitress sighed and wiped her hands on her apron. "Be back in a sec," she said and took off.

Helen looked sideways at Biddle. He rolled his eyes, and she chuckled.

In another minute or two, Velma returned.

"So, where'd I leave off?"

"We were talking about Delilah and her ex-husband," Helen said, steering Velma away from the subject of raising wayward children.

"Oh, yeah, Delilah and Milton." Velma pushed the pencil into her hair. "Sometimes you'd have thought from the way Dee talked that she was still half in love with him. Mostly, though, she just hated his guts. She said he'd screwed her out of what he owed her after they'd split. And when she got wind of him selling that riverfront land to the water park for all that bread." Velma blew out a breath. "Look out."

"She knew about the land deal from the get-go?" Biddle asked.

"Who didn't?" Velma shrugged. "I mean, it was big news in the paper. Every time there was a protest, the *Telegraph* had a front-page story. Delilah couldn't miss the headlines, not with folks reading at the counter while they shoveled in their eggs and bacon. It made her furious, knowing the old man was getting a fortune when she'd had to raise those boys alone on next to nothing."

"She threatened to get a lawyer," Helen said, remembering what Delilah had told her after the funeral service. "Maybe she figured with the land deal, she could finally get him to pay up."

"Oh, she had big dreams all right." Velma sighed. "When she learned Milton sealed the deal with Wet 'n' Woolly, it lit a fire under her. She was married to him when his pop died and left him those acres. She thought half of it should be hers or the kids anyway. She was on the phone a lot these last few weeks. It had Hank pretty pissed off. He told her to take care of her personal crap after work, not during."

Helen glanced at Biddle but he was busy scribbling in his notepad.

"Did Delilah ever hire that lawyer?" she asked.

"She mouthed off a lot about it mostly and then something happened," Velma said but interrupted herself with a chirpy, "More coffee?" At Helen's nod, she perfunctorily refilled the cup then continued. "She suddenly got quiet about Milton. When I asked if everything was okay, she told me that she was finally taking care of things with him. I assumed she'd found someone to take her on, maybe one of those fellows from those late-night TV ads."

"Ambulance chasers," Biddle mumbled as he tore into a second doughnut.

Helen thought of a line from Shakespeare at that moment, one from the second act of Henry VI: *The first thing we do, let's kill all the lawyers . . .*

She stifled her smile and asked Velma, "Did she meet with anyone here in the restaurant last week before her husband's death?"

"I wouldn't say she met up with anyone." Velma paused, hands on hips. She scratched at her hairnet. "But Delilah turned white as a sheet during lunch the week before last. I thought she'd seen a ghost sitting at one of her tables. I heard her say, 'aw, hell, what'd I do to deserve this?' But then she tossed that red hair of hers and glued a smile on her face like nothing happened."

"You know a name?" Biddle asked.

"Sorry."

"Can you give us a description?"

Velma screwed up her face. "Let's see, middle-aged, curvy. A faded kind of pretty."

"Curvy and pretty?" Helen echoed and pushed away her coffee cup. "So, it was a woman?"

"A blonde." Velma nodded. "Reminded me of Shirley Temple with a bad case of the frizzies."

Helen met Biddle's eyes.

"Velma! Pick up!"

Velma smiled limply. "Off I go again."

"That's quite all right." Biddle hopped down from the stool and fished into his pocket.

"Oh, no, it's on me, Sheriff," Velma said, but Biddle shook his head.

He dropped enough bills on the counter to cover the coffee and doughnuts as well as Velma's tip. "You've been a great help, Miss Simms. Thanks again for your time." He plunked on his hat before taking Helen's arm and rushing her out of the place like it was on fire.

Helen sat quietly in the car as he drove away from the rest stop and onto the highway toward Alton. When she could bear the silence no more, she asked, "Are you thinking what I'm thinking?"

"Yup," Biddle said though he didn't take his gaze off the road.

"My, oh, my," Helen murmured and sank into her seat with a sigh, wondering what the devil was really going on between the two Mrs. Grones.

CHAPTER THIRTY

Once back in River Bend, Biddle pulled the car in front of the dented mailbox that said GRONE in faded white letters.

He shut off the ignition but didn't get out. Instead, he stared through the windshield at the broken-down house, frowning. "What do you think of this whole set-up?" he asked Helen.

She followed his gaze, looking at the patched screened door in the center of the rickety porch. "I haven't a clue," she confessed. "I had the impression that Delilah and Shotsie despised one another. If that's not the case then they certainly put on quite a show."

The sheriff patted the steering wheel. "I've got dozens of townsfolk who'll testify to seeing Shotsie Grone at the town meeting the night Milton was killed."

"I saw her there myself," Helen said, though something about that night, something someone had mentioned recently, nagged at her brain. What was it, she wondered? She even closed her eyes, trying to jog her memory, but only drew a blank. She sighed. It would come to her eventually. It always did. She just had to be patient.

"From what Miss Simms said, it looks like Delilah might have made it to River Bend earlier than she'd like us to believe," the sheriff said. "That makes her alibi awful shaky." He scratched at his chin. "If only Milton could talk."

"You know a good medium, Sheriff?"

He smiled thinly at her teasing. "It's time I got a straight answer from Mrs. Grone. The *both* of them," he hastily added.

"So now they're suspects?"

Biddle reached for the door handle then paused. "Hell, Mrs. Evans, I've got too many suspects to count on one hand." He glanced at her. "What does your Spidey-sense tell you about Milt's women?"

Helen had been pondering that all the way back from the truck stop. "What if they were meeting behind Milton's back to try to work things out?"

Biddle raised his eyebrows.

"Maybe Shotsie was tired of Delilah haranguing Milt about the money he owed her," she suggested. "Shotsie confided in me yesterday that she and Milton had been fighting a lot lately. She could have promised Delilah that she'd pay her off once the land deal went through, just to get her off their backs."

"Okay," the sheriff said, "I'll admit that's plausible enough. But if their getting together was so innocent, why did they keep it a secret once Milton was dead? Why did they continue to act like they hated each other's guts?"

"Perhaps, because they do."

"You've got a point," he replied, getting out of the car.

Helen followed him up the cracked walkway to the front door. As he knocked, she noted a beat-up pickup truck in the graveled drive to their right.

Biddle banged some more before Shotsie appeared on the other side of the screen, looking disheveled and notably perturbed.

"Good Lord, Sheriff," she said through the mesh. "And Mrs. Evans, too?" She made no move to invite them in. "What do y'all want *this* time?"

Biddle doffed his hat, turning it around in his hands. "I've got some new information in your husband's case that I need to discuss."

"Is she gonna eavesdrop?" Shotsie asked, jerking a thumb at Helen.

"If I make you uneasy, I can go," Helen said.

"You can stay," Shotsie said but her frown remained. "I've got nothing to hide. Cripes, the whole town can listen as far as I'm concerned." She pushed the screened door wide and gestured impatiently. "Let's get this over with."

Helen sat beside Sheriff Biddle on a lumpy sofa upholstered in a green and brown plaid. Shotsie perched with crossed arms and legs on a lime-colored club chair, her posture decidedly unfriendly. "What's this new information you've got?" she asked. "I hope it's that you've arrested Felicity Timmons, the old bag."

Helen bristled but stayed mum.

The sheriff cleared his throat, setting down his hat on the scratched coffee table. He plucked the black notebook from his breast pocket and rifled through a few pages, finding a clean one. Then he retrieved his pen and clicked on the point. "Before I tell you what I know, I'd appreciate if you'd explain the extent of your relationship with the first Mrs. Grone."

"The extent of my what?" Shotsie snapped.

"How close are you and Delilah?" Helen asked, putting it as simply as possible. "Do you see her often?"

"Do I see Milt's first wife?" she repeated, her back stiffening. She stared unblinking, then threw back her head and snorted. "If I had my way, I'd send Delilah to the moon, okay? She makes me sick from the top of her bottle-dyed red head to the toes of her ridiculous stilettos."

"Do you deny going to see her at her workplace?" Biddle inquired.

"What, you think I dropped by the truck stop to chat and have lunch?" Shotsie said, not answering the question.

"I'll ask again, Mrs. Grone," Biddle said, sounding tense, "Did you or did you not go to Delilah's workplace and sit at her station the week before Milton was killed?"

Shotsie pressed her plump mouth closed, toying with a yellow curl and staring off into space. Finally, she shook her head. "Nope," she told them. "Not that I can remember."

Helen and the sheriff exchanged a knowing glance. He didn't look as though he believed the woman any more than Helen did. They had caught her in a bald-faced lie.

"That's funny," the sheriff said and licked the pad of his finger to flip to a specific page in his notebook. "Because I spoke to Delilah's co-worker this morning, and she swears she saw a woman who looks exactly like you sitting in Delilah's station mere days before Milton's death."

Shotsie paled. "That's not true," she said, her voice sounded smaller than usual. "Someone's making up stories. Maybe it's Delilah. She always had it in for me, the witch."

"Stop playing games, Mrs. Grone." Biddle shut the black notebook and slapped it on his thigh. "I know you met with Milton's ex-wife behind his back, and, if you won't explain why, I'll have to assume you were planning his murder."

"What? No!" Shotsie uncrossed her arms, waving them at Biddle. "It wasn't like that at all! Delilah wouldn't leave us alone. She kept calling and nagging. Miltie was ready to explode! Once Delilah knew about Wet 'n' Woolly, it only got worse." Shotsie fidgeted like a restless child. "She was on him like a tick. She refused to let go. Then she told him she'd tie up that land deal in court for ages if he didn't pay up. She claimed half of it was rightly hers 'cause they were married when he inherited."

Now they were getting somewhere, Helen thought. That certainly fit with what Velma had told them this morning.

Shotsie chewed on a fingernail. "Milt acted like he didn't take Delilah seriously. Heck, he was too busy screwing around with the pastor's daughter to care. But I was worried enough for the both of us." Shotsie's expression turned hard. "Then Miltie got himself killed and that was all there was to it." She looked at Biddle. "Are you gonna throw me in jail for that, Sheriff? Is it against the law in River Bend to try to help your own husband?"

Oh, boy, Helen thought, as Biddle squared his shoulders.

Helen wondered if he found Shotsie's story plausible. Thank goodness it wasn't Helen's call. She had no idea what to believe.

The sheriff tucked away his notebook and pen. Hands firmly on his knees, he leaned toward Shotsie. "Did you see Delilah Grone last Thursday night?"

"Me?" Shotsie's eyes widened. "I told you, Sheriff, I went to the town meeting at seven o'clock. Miltie was cleaning his shotgun when I left. I walked alone to town hall. If Delilah was around, I didn't run into her."

"She came to River Bend to talk to Milton," Biddle said. "She claims he was dead when she got here but there's a slight problem with the timeline."

"Well, isn't that something." A deep pink tinged Shotsie's cheeks. "So, she was here that night. Maybe she's the one who hit him. She probably figured she had a better chance of getting his money if he was dead."

"But she's not even in his will," Helen said, repeating the gossip she'd heard from Milton's lawyer's wife.

"I guess she just hated him that much," Shotsie declared. "She could have shown up here after I left for town hall. Maybe she and Miltie fought, and she grabbed Mrs. Timmons' shovel, whacking him in the head and taking off."

"Slow down there, Mrs. Grone." Biddle scratched his brow. "I thought you were convinced that Felicity Timmons was the killer?"

Shotsie nibbled on a fingernail. "They could've been in it together. Maybe the old bat left that shovel out so it'd be handy for Delilah to grab."

"Heavens to Betsy," Helen said and rolled her eyes. This was getting downright silly. If Shotsie had her way, Biddle would be locking up Felicity, Earnest Fister, and Milton's ex-wife together.

"We might be getting just a little off-track, ma'am," Biddle said, looking flustered.

As far as Helen was concerned, they were done. She nudged his shin with the toe of her sneaker, hoping he'd get the message.

"Right," he said and rose, picking up his hat. "I think that about does it. Thank you for your time, Mrs. Grone. I'll be in touch."

Shotsie nipped at their heels as Biddle and Helen made a beeline for the door. "What about Delilah? Aren't you going to do something?"

"She's on my list," the sheriff said. "I aim to talk to her today."

They'd nearly reached the car when Shotsie yelled from the stoop, "Hey, if you need me again, you'd better call first! This isn't an Amtrak station!"

Biddle waved in reply then got into the car in a hurry.

Helen hadn't even clicked her seatbelt when he started the engine. The squad car jerked into motion, and they rolled past Felicity's Victorian, the gravel crunching beneath the tires.

Helen sat in silence.

"You've got something on your mind, ma'am, something you're not telling me?" Biddle asked.

"Do I?" she murmured.

"I wish you'd share it with me, Mrs. Evans."

Helen didn't have anything to tell him, not yet, nothing concrete. "I've always liked crossword puzzles," she said, not meaning to sound cryptic. "Once you find a few key words here and there, the others just fall into place."

"Crossword puzzles?" He chortled. "What's that got to do with Milton Grone?"

"Oh, you'd be surprised," she murmured, the murky answer becoming clearer in her own mind. She only wondered why she hadn't seen it sooner.

CHAPTER THIRTY-ONE

Madeline Fister sprawled across the sofa, feet propped up on its scroll-arm, pointing the remote and clicking through channels with lethal precision.

Game show.

Zap.

Soap opera.

Zap.

Talk show.

Zap.

Finally, she switched the set off altogether. Tossing aside the remote, she got up. She was bored out of her skull.

Stay inside, Maddy. Take it easy, Maddy. Relax until you're better, Maddy.

Her father's voice played over and over in her head like a song set on endless repeat. When would he ever stop treating her like a child? When would he realize she could take care of herself without him butting in and ruining everything?

Her eyes blurred, and she roughly wiped away the tears.

If only your mother were here. If only Mom could talk to you now. If only she could see what you've done.

Stop it!

Maddy pressed her hands to her ears and shook her head. She didn't want her mother to see how she'd turned out. She'd disappoint her. She'd make her anything but proud.

Why had she done it? Had she needed attention so much? Had she felt so unloved?

She pictured her father standing at the pulpit in his robes, that thick church Bible in-hand, frowning at her with blatant disapproval. In his eyes, she was never good enough. It didn't matter what she did. She always failed.

Don't you understand, Daddy, she wanted to ask him? *Don't you see why I did it?*

Her father loved the church more than her. He held that Bible closer than he'd ever held her. Milton Grone had been just the opposite. He couldn't stop looking at her. He'd sit there by the river, not bothering her. Just glancing over now and then as she tossed rocks into the water and tried to think and forget and just *breathe*. She'd finally walked over to him one day and asked why he stared. "How can I not?" he'd replied. "You're the prettiest thing I ever saw. Even prettier than your mama, and she was a beauty." Maddie hadn't cared that he was older. He looked like George Clooney on those coffee commercials, only not as fancy. Approachable. When Milt had flirted with her, Maddy hadn't discouraged him. In fact, she'd done just the opposite.

Then her father found out and stepped right in between them. He couldn't let Maddy live her own life or make her own choices.

And now look what he'd done! Look at the mess he'd made of it all!

Maddy struggled into her high-top sneakers, roughly tugging at the laces, tying them so tightly the canvas cut through her flimsy socks and into the skin at her ankles.

She had to get out for a bit. She needed to escape this stuffy house crammed with her father's things: the crosses and pictures of Jesus that hung on the walls; the religious magazines and books; and, most especially, that stupid Bible perched imperiously atop a cloth-covered set of drawers. Her father had found it in the chapel when he'd taken over last year, and it was never far from him. He cradled it in his arms like it was his baby.

Her gaze lingered there, and she swallowed.

Her father kept crisp twenties tucked in an envelope between the pages. Maddy had found them when she'd been poking around one day. On occasion, she'd help herself to a few bills, especially when her allowance fell short. If her dad had noticed, he'd never said a word. Maddy figured he didn't pay enough attention to anything besides his ministry to realize what she did and how often she did it.

Except when it came to Milton Grone.

She pressed her lips together and crossed the room in several quick steps. She pushed open the book, smelling the musty old-age as she flipped through the pages, ignoring the prick of her conscience that told her what she was doing was wrong.

But Maddy didn't care. When her father had stolen Milton away from her, he'd been in the wrong, too.

The last time she'd taken money, the envelope had been stashed away in the Psalms. She found it lodged in the Corinthians now. She plucked it out, her eyes falling upon a highlighted passage: "Love is patient and kind: love is not arrogant or boastful."

Fingers trembling, she stuffed the envelope in her pocket and closed the book.

She left the house without writing a note, something her dad was always after her to do. Let him wonder where she went. Maddy always knew where *he* was: at the chapel.

He was probably working on next Sunday's sermon. He might be there for hours, scribbling away, oblivious to time and to *her* until it was so late that he'd missed dinner. Maddy ate alone lots of times and didn't see her dad until after dark.

She hurried down the sidewalk, figuring she should cut through the woods to avoid bumping into her father, just in case he decided to come home for lunch.

She'd barely walked a block when something made her hesitate, and she looked up.

Across the unpaved road stood a forlorn-looking house, the yard choked with weeds; the windows drawn and dark.

A horrible sadness filled her chest.

She closed her eyes and saw Milton.

She had gone by the day before he died. No, she corrected herself, the day before he was murdered. She'd waited until she saw Shotsie drive off and then she'd banged on the door. He hadn't been happy at all to see her, even less so when she'd told him she was pregnant. Maddy had lost it, crying and begging him to leave his wife, but he'd said it was too late, that it was over. He said her daddy knew, and it had to stop. That he could go to jail, because of her age. She'd been so caught up in bawling and begging that she'd never heard the truck come back. She never heard the footsteps on the porch or the slap of the screened door.

If it hadn't been for Milt, she would have still been standing there in the bedroom when Shotsie walked in.

He'd pushed open the window and shoved her out, calling to his wife all the while, "That you, Shots? Did you forget somethin'?"

"Hello, Madeline."

Maddy jumped, her eyes flying wide open.

Heart pounding, Maddy blinked at the woman in the straw hat who stood behind the nearby fence.

"My dear, are you well?"

Maddy stammered, "I–I'm fine," but her mouth was so dry, her tongue so thick, the words sounded unintelligible even to herself.

Before Felicity Timmons could say any more, Maddy took off running past houses and trees, not stopping to catch her breath until she reached the short stretch of Main Street.

Head hanging, she ducked into a shop with a pink awning, setting the bell to jingling as she entered. "Francine's Fashions," read a sign just inside the place. "Shoplifters will be prosecuted. Have a nice day."

"Oh, it's you, Miss Fister," the store's owner, Francine — who happened to be the mayor's daughter — said from behind the sales counter. "Take your time and look around."

Madeline glanced over and saw the way the woman stared at her, probably thinking to herself, "Oh, dear, it's the minister's wild child. I hope I don't have to pat her down on her way out."

She circumvented racks of polyester pantsuits and cotton knits with collars up to there, ending up in the rear where teenaged fashions shared space with maternity wear.

"Can I help you find anything in particular?" Francine's thin voice chirped from over Madeline's shoulder.

"No."

"Well, if you should need me, I'll be right over here."

Fine! Maddy wanted to scream. *Just leave me alone!*

She ignored the woman until she went away.

Maddy plowed through the meager selection, feeling calmer by the moment. Shopping always cheered her up. She got a little thrill when she bought a new mini-skirt, knowing how her father hated them; or a string bikini in the summer, another item he despised. Using the Bible money made it even more fun.

Though today, for some reason, she just felt guilty. Maybe she wasn't trying hard enough.

She pulled a pair of purple skin-tight jeans off the rack, not caring about the size or color. She marched up to the counter and plunked down the pants, digging into her back pocket for the envelope.

"Don't you want to try them on?" Francine asked, removing the pin that held on the price tag.

"No." Maddy avoided her eyes.

"If you're sure . . ."

"I am."

"Okay, then." Francine pushed several buttons on the register. "That'll be twenty-nine ninety-five."

Maddy nodded, peeling back the flap on the envelope. She snatched out one piece of paper and gave it to Francine.

"Um, I can hardly take that in payment, Miss Fister. Francine's Fashions doesn't deal in used stationery."

Confused, Madeline looked down at her hand and saw what she was holding. It certainly wasn't a crisp, green

Benjamin. It was a letter folded to the size of a dollar-bill. Its surface was covered with cramped writing that appeared unreadable at first glance.

"Oh, God, I'm sorry." Maddy's cheeks burned. Ashamed, she pushed her way out of the shop, the paper clutched in her fist, tears clouding her vision.

She rounded the corner of the building and pressed her back against the brick. Wiping tears on her sleeve, she took a deep breath, all the while wondering what she had taken from the Bible. Had her father stashed away a letter from her mother? Near the end, her mother could hardly speak much less write in a way that was legible.

That was all the motivation Maddy needed.

She unfolded the letterhead, spotting a date from a decade before. She realized instantly that it wasn't her mother's hand or even her father's. In another second, Maddy knew why.

"I, Gerald Grone, being of sound mind and body, here and now admit this document, witnessed by the honorable Reverend Jeremiah Jones and his wife Winifred, as a legal codicil to my will."

Oh, my God.

Maddy swallowed.

She pushed away from the building, hurrying up the sidewalk. She held the letter up to her eyes, reading as she walked.

"In accordance with the laws of the state, I do so designate that the fifty acres of land situated in the River Bend Valley shall be bequeathed to the town of River Bend upon my death, to do with as they please."

Maddy's brain raced as swiftly as her feet.

This was how her father did it, she realized. It wasn't the threats of calling the sheriff that had kept Milt away! No wonder he'd told her their relationship was over. No wonder he'd refused to leave his wife!

Fury shot through her veins and her eyes so filled with tears that she didn't see what was ahead of her until it was too late. She ran into him head-first, and he grunted loudly. Knocked off-balance, she would have fallen had he not caught her by the arms.

"Maddy!" his familiar voice barked. "What are you doing? Why in heaven are you out? Didn't I tell you stay at home?"

She gazed into her dad's bearded face, into the furrowed brow and dark eyes that bore into her soul. Then she pushed away, shoved as hard as she could, until he let her go.

Backing up a step, she stared at him. "How could you?" she asked, her voice rising. Her pulse throbbed in her temples. "How could you do it?" she said again, thrusting out her hand, shaking the letter at him.

He looked puzzled and, she thought, frightened as well. He silently took the page she pressed at him. He glanced at it and shook his head. "This has nothing to do with you."

"Doesn't it?" she cried.

"He would never have married you anyway, don't you see that?"

"He never had the chance," Maddy said even if the tiny voice inside her wondered if he was right.

"I never wanted you to know."

She hugged her arms around herself, shivering uncontrollably. "Well, I do now, Daddy. I figured it out. You blackmailed him to make him stay away from me."

He held his palms out in surrender. "I did it for you, Madeline," he told her in a whisper she could hardly hear. "I'd do it again, if I had to."

"Did you kill him?" she asked, speaking aloud what she'd only imagined before, what she'd feared most of all. "Did you do it to keep us apart for good?"

He flinched, and she saw how much she'd hurt him by her question. Still, when he didn't answer, she said once more. "*Did you*?"

He shook his head, eyes downcast. "No," he told her. "But if it had come to it, if there had been no other way—" He lifted his chin. "I can't honestly tell you I wouldn't have. I thought of it enough."

She bit down on her lip, stunned by his words, unsure of what she'd expected to hear.

"I love you, Maddy," he said, sounding so afraid, so unlike the confident pastor who took to the pulpit every Sunday morning, such control in his actions, his voice. "There's nothing I wouldn't do to protect you."

"You have to tell them. You can't keep this a secret forever."

"I know." He stared at the paper. His hands shook.

"It was wrong what you did."

"Will you never let me make it right?"

She looked at him closely, at the gray in his beard, the lines around his mouth and eyes, and she was suddenly a little girl again, wanting his affection so desperately, needing his attention; always trying to come up with something to take him away from his work, from his parishioners who stole so much of his time.

She must have made life as difficult for him as she made it for herself. To do what he'd done, to blackmail someone, it defied everything he stood for. But he'd done it for her, regardless. How could she have been so blind?

"Oh, Daddy!"

He put his arms around her, and she allowed him to hold her.

"It'll be all right," he was saying, as he had again and again ever since her mom died. "It'll be all right."

Only, this time, she believed him.

CHAPTER THIRTY-TWO

Helen waved as Biddle's dusty patrol car pulled away from her front walk. She waited until it turned the corner and disappeared from her sight. Then, she did an about-face, heading in the same direction from whence they'd come.

She followed her instincts and the sidewalk, ending up at Felicity's house barely ten minutes after.

Noting the absence of her friend's brown sedan in the carport, Helen cut across the perfectly-groomed yard to the back patio. There, in the shade of overhanging elms and oaks, she settled onto a cushioned wrought iron chair and waited.

When twenty minutes passed, she feared her intuition might have failed her.

After another five, she sighed and got up.

Stepping over the monkey grass that bordered the patio, she heard the noise of a car approaching and froze.

She peered through the leaves of a rhododendron as a green automobile lurched up to the intersection and turned right, spewing gravel as it raced around the corner at a speed surpassed only, Helen thought, by the morning paperboy.

With a sputter and succession of loud backfires, the car tucked in behind the pickup parked in the driveway next door.

Helen smiled, though not from amusement, rather from simply knowing that her gut had been right.

She watched the driver get out and clatter up the porch steps, banging on the frame of the screened door with both fists. Without waiting for an answer, she let herself in.

Helen hurried across Felicity's lawn and squatted through the split-rail fence, creeping up to the side of the house, wincing at the groan of the stairs as she ascended the dilapidated stoop.

She paused at the screened door, listening to the clash of voices coming from within. Some of it was too garbled to make out, though most she heard loud and clear.

"You're trying to pin this on me now, are you, Shots? How dare you tell the sheriff that I'm guilty when you're the one who got me into this mess in the first place!" the first Mrs. Grone ranted, obviously learning of Sheriff Biddle's visit from Milton's widow. She sounded mad enough to choke a horse.

Shotsie's reply was no less vehement. "What else was I supposed to do, huh? He knew I'd gone down to the truck stop to talk to you before Miltie kicked the bucket. Your brainless co-worker spilled the beans! Did you want me to tell him the truth?"

Rapid-fire curses ensued, the words flying back and forth so fast Helen couldn't make out which woman said what. Before Helen had a chance to scoot, the door flew open and Delilah burst out. Helen grabbed for the handrail to keep from falling off the porch.

"What the—" Delilah caught herself and did a double-take. "Mrs. Evans?" Her whole face turned red despite the make-up that coated her skin. "What're you doing here?"

Helen tried to come up with a quick and believable pretense. But she changed her mind, deciding that it was time someone told the truth around here. "I figured Shotsie might phone you after the sheriff and I left," she said, "and that you'd drive up from Alton as soon as you heard."

"What's going on?" The screened door flapped open, and Shotsie emerged. "Oh, it's you," she said, spying Helen. "So how much did you hear, you old busybody?"

"Shut your fat mouth for a minute and maybe she'll tell us," Delilah spat over her shoulder. "Maybe we should go inside."

"I'm comfortable out here," Helen said.

"That's too bad," Delilah replied and grabbed her arm, holding tight. "Because I think we'd be more comfortable indoors."

Helen thought about screaming for help but she hadn't seen anyone else around. She didn't want to believe the women would hurt her besides. They were in enough trouble as it was, and Frank Biddle would figure things out sooner or later. Definitely sooner if they tossed another dead body into the mix.

"Sit down," Delilah told her, dragging Helen into the living room and pushing her toward the ugly plaid couch, the very place where she and the sheriff had sat only half an hour before.

Delilah settled in the green club chair across from her.

Shotsie stood with her hands on her hips, glowering. "Say what's on your mind, you nosy Nellie," she grumbled, her face a puffy mask of indignation. "I swear, I've had enough of you and the sheriff and everyone else in this stupid town. I should sue you all for harassment!"

"Would you close your freakin' pie hole and let the lady speak?" Delilah countered.

"Are you talkin' to me?"

"Who else has a pie hole that won't shut?"

"Why, you bit—!"

"*Shut up*!"

Helen listened to them throw insults back and forth and shook her head. She was certain now more than ever that the two really did despise each other. The scene they'd caused at Milton's funeral wasn't an act at all. They deeply and sincerely hated each other's guts.

She shifted in her seat, suddenly doubting herself. What if her theory wasn't right? What if she'd jumped to conclusions?

No. She didn't see as how it could have happened any other way.

"I know what you did," she said loudly enough to be heard over their shouting match. "I know how you killed Milton."

Abruptly, their argument ceased.

Shotsie narrowed her eyes. "This should be good," she said and began twisting a yellow curl around her finger. "I like made-up stories."

"Quiet," Delilah hissed at Shotsie. "Go on, Mrs. Evans. For once I agree with the Black Widow."

Helen set her hands in her lap. "It did take me awhile to put the pieces together," she said. "The clues were right there in front of me the whole time, though I didn't see them at first. Then little by little, I figured out how they fit. It began with a slip of the tongue here, an off-the-cuff remark there, an observation that made no sense until now."

The women stared at her, silent for once.

Helen wet her lips. "I must say this plan of yours was very clever. You might have gotten away with it, too, if you hadn't left so many telltale crumbs in your wake."

"What plan?" Shotsie sniffed. "I think you've had one too many bad prunes, if you don't mind my sayin'."

Delilah flipped brassy hair over her shoulder, feigning nonchalance. But Helen saw the worry in her eyes and the creases in her brow that were deeper than a moment before. "What exactly do you think you know?" she asked.

"You lied to me, Mrs. Grone," Helen said to the redhead. "You claimed not to have arrived in town until after Milton was dead, right before the crowd from town hall descended on this house. But Velma Simms said you ducked out before your shift ended at seven."

She paused, remembering something the sheriff had mentioned in passing while they'd driven to the truck stop. It had to do with his questioning Maddy Fister.

"The backfire from your car," she remarked, "it sounds like fireworks."

"So?"

"The pastor's daughter heard three or four pops before the chapel bell tolled at eight. She assumed it had come from the cop show she'd been watching when she'd dozed off." Helen shook her head. "But the pops didn't come from the TV. They came from your car."

If Delilah registered shock at the revelation, she hid it well. She didn't even twitch. Instead, she settled back in the club chair and crossed her legs. "That doesn't prove anything, Mrs. Evans. It just means that I was in River Bend that night, like I said, and that I saw Milton dead before anyone else."

"Velma Simms saw Shotsie at the truck stop during your shift before Milton was murdered," Helen said.

"You're reaching, grandma." Shotsie pulled a face. "There's no law against two ex-wives meeting up for a chat. Don't make it sound like we plotted together to do in Miltie."

"You said it, Mrs. Grone," Helen murmured, "not I."

Delilah started laughing. "My God," she said, fighting to catch her breath, brushing tears from her eyes. "That's the biggest load of crap I've ever heard. The two of us kill Milt? Why? I'm not even in his will so why do I care?"

"Yes, you did mention it to me, didn't you?" Helen nodded. "Just as the current Mrs. Grone made a point of attending the meeting in town hall and convincing all of River Bend that she knew next to nothing about Milton's haul from the Wet 'n' Woolly deal."

"She's the one who had everything to gain," Delilah said, hooking a thumb at Shotsie. "I had nothing to gain by killing Milton. Nothing."

"Oh, but you did." Helen insisted. "You must've realized that as long as Milt lived, you'd never get that money he owed you. With his windfall from the water park, he could've tied you up in court for years. It was a good bet you wouldn't see any of that back alimony or child support, not as long as he was around to fight."

"But by murdering him I would?" Delilah said dryly.

"There was always a chance your children would inherit something or that his estate might pay up what you were owed in the end." Her eyes went from the ex-Mrs. Grone to his widow and back again. "It surely couldn't hurt that his likely beneficiary was a woman you were in cahoots with and who probably promised you some type of compensation once Milton was dead."

"Horse hockey!" Shotsie's face turned bright red. "If I'd wanted Miltie gone, why didn't I just divorce him? I'll tell you why! Because I loved him. You hear me? I loved him in spite of everything he'd done!"

"That may have been true once," Helen acknowledged, not doubting Shotsie's declaration. "But learning that he'd messed around with Madeline Fister was the straw that broke the camel's back, was it not? You admitted that you knew. In fact, you told me more than you should have," she said, watching Shotsie's pink cheeks turn bloodless. "I figure you had to overhear Milton talking to Madeline. That's the only way you could have known she was pregnant unless he told you himself. Until just recently, no one besides the pastor and his daughter knew for certain who the father was except you and Milton."

"You're crazy," Shotsie hissed.

"You were afraid that if Milt left you for Madeline, you'd end up in the same fix as Delilah," Helen continued, unable to turn back once she'd gone this far. "You feared Milton might abandon you for a young woman, like he abandoned his own children. If he did, you'd be left with nothing, just like Delilah. And with all that money he'd be coming into because of the land he sold . . ."

"Liar!" Shotsie shouted, shaking a finger at Helen. "Those are lies, every word. No one's gonna believe you. You're old and batty. You might even have dementia."

Helen took a deep breath and looked at Delilah who'd pulled a cigarette out of her purse. But her red-tipped fingers shook too much to light it. "You had plenty of help from Milton's first wife. She knew about his bad heart, something he never intended for his younger second bride to find out."

"Please!" Delilah tossed the unlit cigarette to the floor. "Lots of folks around here knew about Milt's heart condition. His dad died of heart failure, too. It wasn't a secret."

"No, it wasn't a secret to most," Helen agreed. "But it was to Shotsie. You encouraged her to attend the town meeting that night," she said, looking at Milt's second wife. "You lived here for years. You realized it would give her the perfect alibi."

"Well, I *was* at the meeting," Shotsie said, and her shoulders relaxed. She lifted her chin, looking suddenly confident. "Everybody saw me. I've got dozens of witnesses, at least. No one's got a tighter alibi than me."

That's what had puzzled Helen the most. She'd seen Shotsie in town hall last Thursday night with her own eyes. She thought of Harry Houdini and Blackstone and their genius with slight of hand. Magicians knew how easily the eyes could deceive the senses. A remark of Bebe Horn's over cards last night had made her realize just how much that was true. Even though so many townsfolk had seen Shotsie in attendance, Helen knew of none who'd actually watched her enter.

Helen exhaled slowly, cocking her head as she looked at Grone's widow. "As best I can figure, you must've slipped in late, like Delilah at the funeral service, only you didn't want to make as loud an entrance. Once Art Beaner banged his gavel and Clara started reading the minutes, no one noticed anything else. But I'll wager if the sheriff checked with any late-comers, they'll realize they didn't see you until you stood up and started arguing with Ida." Helen heard her voice shake, but she didn't stop. "I'll admit it was a smart move, Shotsie, drawing attention to yourself as you did." She smiled. "Even I believed you didn't know the money involved in Milton's land deal."

"What a bunch of malarky!" Shotsie's eyes darted to Delilah then back to Helen. "I think you've lost your mind, Mrs. Evans. Just like that batty Felicity Timmons."

"Ah, yes, Felicity," Helen said, tackling another point that had bothered her. "You mentioned more than once watching Felicity plant from dawn to dusk so you knew she kept gardening tools outdoors. Did you get the idea to use her shovel when you saw her argue with your husband that morning?"

"Maybe you should just stop talking," Shotsie snapped.

"You were very quick to suggest to the sheriff that Felicity was guilty and that her missing shovel might be the weapon. But then you had to make sure he'd *find* it. So, you kept badgering him about Felicity until he poked around—"

"Stop!" Shotsie stood right in front of Helen and raised her clenched fists. "Just stop it before I—"

"What?" Helen said, trying to stay calm despite the prickle of fear at the back of her neck. "Are you going to kill me, too? If that's the case, I hope you have a better plan than the one you two concocted for Milton. You don't think I'm the only one who's added it all up?" she told them, hoping she wasn't bluffing. "The sheriff's onto you, too."

"It wasn't me! I didn't hit him!" Shotsie shouted. "It was Delilah! She snuck up on him and *bam*!" The woman shuddered and covered her face with her hands.

Delilah shot out of the chair, grabbing Shotsie by the arms. "Just what the hell are you trying to do here? Throw me under the bus?"

Shotsie glared through her tears. "I'm telling the truth."

"You're trying to save your butt by handing over mine!"

"But you killed him!" Shotsie cried out and twisted away from Delilah. "You banged the shovel down on his head. I saw you do it!" The tear-stained face turned to Helen. "I told Milt I was leaving for town hall, but I doubled back and waited for Delilah. I banged around the garbage cans then hid when he came out. That's when Delilah smacked him with the shovel, and I cut through a bunch of backyards to get to the meeting."

"Shut your damned mouth!" Delilah teetered on her high heels. She was shaking like a leaf. "How dare you put this on me when I was the one who lured him out and you did the hitting—"

"Me?"

"Yes, you!"

"It was her idea, all of it," Shotsie sobbed. "She's the one who came to me with the scheme, and I was so mad at Miltie for sleeping with that girl that I was willing to do anything so I wouldn't be left with nothing. I don't want to work at a truck stop for the rest of my life!"

Helen got to her feet, less concerned for her own safety now than for what Delilah might do to Shotsie. "Mrs. Grone," she said to one and then to the other, "Mrs. Grone, please, let's all stop and take a breath, okay?"

"You conniving little worm!" Delilah shoved Shotsie, who stumbled to the floor. "It was your idea to kill Milton! You kept babbling on and on about how good things would be if only Milt was out of the picture."

"Ladies, please," Helen tried again.

Shotsie picked herself up from the rug, screaming, "Murderer!"

"Killer!" Delilah yelled right back.

Then they went at each other for real. Delilah grabbed for Shotsie's hair and Shotsie for Delilah's.

Helen backed away, knowing she'd never pry them apart without getting pulled into the fray. And, at her age, she was too old for fisticuffs. Just watching the two Mrs. Grones wrestle made her bones start to ache.

She hurried up the hallway to the safety of the kitchen. From there, she phoned the sheriff, telling him to get to the Grones' house ASAP.

An ear-piercing scream rent the air, and she put a hand to her breast, her heart pounding.

She dug around in the pantry and found what she wanted in a cobwebbed corner. Armed with a broom, she swallowed hard and marched toward the caterwauling, wondering if it was any more trouble to break up a human cat fight than an honest-to-goodness feline one.

CHAPTER THIRTY-THREE

"So, they killed him for nothing?" Helen said, squinting at the handwritten codicil to Gerald Grone's will that she held at an arm's length. She'd had Biddle read her its contents just a minute before, something she would have done herself if she hadn't left her glasses on the porch with her crossword.

"It appears that way, ma'am."

"But where was the codicil all this time?" Helen asked, tapping a finger to the page. "And how on earth did Earnest Fister find it?"

Biddle shifted in his chair. "It seems he discovered it weeks ago. He claims it was stuck in that old desk he's been using in the chapel. He'd had to force a drawer open when it jammed, and he ending up pulling the whole thing to the floor." Biddle shrugged. "He knew the significance the moment he read it. He nearly turned it over to the board but then he realized he had a better use for it."

Helen sighed. "Blackmailing Milton Grone."

"Well, it worked. It kept the old man away from his daughter."

Helen pursed her lips. "So, who do you think actually did it, Sheriff? Shotsie or Delilah?"

Biddle scratched his unshaven jaw. "I'll let the county prosecutors sort that one out, Mrs. Evans. I just hope they stash 'em in separate cells, or else there might not be enough left of either of them to put on the stand."

Helen smiled thinly. "They're quite a pair, aren't they? They nearly got away with murder. If Velma hadn't spotted them together at the truck spot, we might never have known."

Biddle cleared his throat. "Um, ma'am?"

"Yes?"

"You know my crack about your having a Miss Marple complex, well, um, I think I should apologize."

"No need," Helen said, waving him off. "I'm just grateful that Felicity's not the one sitting in jail instead of those two."

Biddle coughed and busied himself with some papers on his desk.

Helen tapped the codicil. "Do you imagine this will hold up in court, even against Wet 'n' Woolly?"

"I already had a talk with Stanley Horn," Biddle said, leaning back and folding his arms atop his belly. "As long as the same number of witnesses to the formal will were present as the codicil was signed, then it has a good chance of being upheld."

"Oh, my gosh," Helen breathed and pressed the page between her hands. "I just thought of something."

"Ma'am?"

"Whatever will happen when Ida Bell gets wind of this? I'd hate to see what she does to the water-park people when she finds she's got a legal leg to stand on."

"God help them, Mrs. Evans."

Helen laughed, and Biddle shook his head.

"God help 'em all."

CHAPTER THIRTY-FOUR

The next day . . .

"Stop this thing! Stop, I say!"

Ida left Dotty's side and abandoned the small band of her sign-toting comrades. Without a thought to her own safety, she ran directly in front of the bulldozer rolling through the knee-high grass.

She dug in her boot heels and waved her arms above her head. "Halt this instant!" she shouted against the noisy groan of the engine. "Halt, I say!"

Above the dozer's loud grunts, she heard the horrified shrieks of her friends and closed her eyes, bracing herself for the worst as the huge machine came at her; its claw-like shovel lowered to the ground as it rumbled ever closer.

Expecting to be lifted off her feet, Ida cracked open an eyelid a minute after when she realized she hadn't moved and the motor was not groaning but idling.

Ida peered ahead and held her breath, realizing that only two feet stood between herself and the big, yellow machine.

The bulldozer operator jumped down from his perch and stomped up to her. "Move it, or I'll run you over!" he yelled, sticking his face into hers so that she felt his spittle hit her skin. "I've got a job to do, you old geezer, and you're all that's keeping me from doing it!"

"Over my dead body!" she shouted, crossing her arms over her chest, unwilling to budge even a fraction.

He shrugged, looking her up and down, as if comparing her to some sapling to be uprooted. "If that's the way you want it."

"You can't do this!"

"Says who?"

"Says the law," she cried happily, shoving her hand into her pants pocket and withdrawing a crumpled piece of paper. It was a cease-and-desist order Sheriff Biddle had gotten from a county judge, thanks to the recently-discovered codicil to Gerald Grone's will. She shook it under his nose. "Now turn that contraption around post haste!"

The dozer operator snatched the paper from her, holding it up with filthy gloves. "Is this on the up and up?" he asked. "Or did you print this up yourself?"

Ida laughed. She'd dealt with disbelievers before.

"It's as real as I am," she said, adding with the shrillness of a drill sergeant, "Stand back and watch this old geezer in action."

She brushed past him and around the lowered shovel, clambering up and behind the dozer's controls without a thought as to the danger. She'd never driven a machine quite like this but figured it wasn't all that different from the combines and tractors she'd learned to drive once upon a time at her father's Jerseyville farm. She fumbled with the gears, whooping when the engine went from idling to growling again.

"Wait a minute, lady! Hey, get down from there!"

But Ida had already pulled the gearshift into motion, sending the bulldozer slowly moving forward. The machine rumbled beneath her like a fire breathing dragon, and Ida felt more powerful than she'd ever felt in her life.

She spotted Dotty staring up, wide-eyed, alongside the handful of others, and she puffed out her breast as exhilaration sped the blood through her veins.

"Tally-ho!" she cried, steering the dozer toward the Wet 'n' Woolly billboard, urging it ahead until the sign was knocked flat on the ground, crushed beneath the rubber-covered crawlers to mere smithereens.

Only then she did stop the bulldozer's rumbling. Throwing back her head, she let out a joyful shout; while, high above her in the trees, all the birds began to sing.

THE END

THE JOFFE BOOKS STORY

We began in 2014 when Jasper agreed to publish his mum's much-rejected romance novel and it became a bestseller.

Since then we've grown into the largest independent publisher in the UK. We're extremely proud to publish some of the very best writers in the world, including Joy Ellis, Faith Martin, Caro Ramsay, Helen Forrester, Simon Brett and Robert Goddard. Everyone at Joffe Books loves reading and we never forget that it all begins with the magic of an author telling a story.

We are proud to publish talented first-time authors, as well as established writers whose books we love introducing to a new generation of readers.

We won Trade Publisher of the Year at the Independent Publishing Awards in 2023. We have been shortlisted for Independent Publisher of the Year at the British Book Awards for the last four years, and were shortlisted for the Diversity and Inclusivity Award at the 2022 Independent Publishing Awards. In 2023 we were shortlisted for Publisher of the Year at the RNA Industry Awards.

We built this company with your help, and we love to hear from you, so please email us about absolutely anything bookish at feedback@joffebooks.com

If you want to receive free books every Friday and hear about all our new releases, join our mailing list: www.joffebooks.com/contact

And when you tell your friends about us, just remember: it's pronounced Joffe as in coffee or toffee!

ALSO BY SUSAN MCBRIDE

HELEN EVANS INVESTIGATES
Book 1: TO HELEN BACK

Printed in Great Britain
by Amazon

40359339R00118